She smoothed her blouse over her hips

Her round, very sexy hips. Damned if D.J. didn't want to pull her close and get back to what they'd started on the dance floor.

No way, he warned himself, and backed up a step. He had enough on his plate. He did not want to get involved with Liza Miller.

"Hey, I understand. You were badly burned and you don't trust guys. That's exactly why I don't get serious. Men and women can't trust each other, and when they fall in love somebody gets hurt."

"Something we both understand," she said.

Then she looked at him. She was just as attracted to him as he was to her...he saw it in her eyes.

Dear Reader,

This is the second book in the Halo Island miniseries and features D. J. Hatcher, pilot and owner of Island Air, and Liza Miller, a recently laid off teacher who grew up on the island.

Liza hasn't been back on Halo Island for three years—since her fiancé left her at the altar. She's back now, to help her grandmother pack and move to a retirement home. She hopes to find a job soon.

Several years ago D.J.'s now-ex wife ran off with his business partner, leaving him in a world of hurt and financial debt that now threatens the company.

Though both D.J. and Liza have trust issues working to push them apart, they manage to fall in love. I hope you like their story as much as I enjoyed writing it.

I welcome your continued e-mails and letters. E-mail me at ann@annroth.net, or write to me at Ann Roth, P.O. Box 25003, Seattle, WA 98165-1903. Please visit my Web site at www.annroth.net, where you'll find my latest writing news and a delicious recipe every month.

Until next time,
Happy reading!

Ann Roth

The Pilot's Woman
ANN ROTH

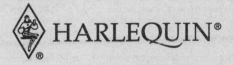

HARLEQUIN®

TORONTO • NEW YORK • LONDON
AMSTERDAM • PARIS • SYDNEY • HAMBURG
STOCKHOLM • ATHENS • TOKYO • MILAN • MADRID
PRAGUE • WARSAW • BUDAPEST • AUCKLAND

Special thanks to Kevin Thomson and Joe Leatherman
at Kenmore Air (Kenmoreair.com). Both of you took
time out of your busy schedules to answer my questions
and take me on a tour of Kenmore Air. Any mistakes or
misinformation are mine.

ISBN-13: 978-0-373-75208-9
ISBN-10: 0-373-75208-3

THE PILOT'S WOMAN

This edition published by arrangement with Harlequin Books S.A.

www.eHarlequin.com

Printed in U.S.A.

ABOUT THE AUTHOR

Ann Roth has always been a voracious reader of everything from classics to mysteries to romance. Of all the books she's read, love stories have affected her the most, and stayed with her the longest. A firm believer in the power of love, Ann enjoys creating emotional stories that illustrate how love can triumph over seemingly insurmountable odds.

Ann lives in the greater Seattle area with her husband and a really irritating cat who expects her breakfast no later than 6:00 a.m., seven days a week.

She would love to hear from readers. You can write her c/o P.O. Box 25003, Seattle WA 98165-1903 or e-mail her at ann@annroth.net.

Books by Ann Roth

HARLEQUIN AMERICAN ROMANCE
1031—THE LAST TIME WE KISSED
1103—THE BABY INHERITANCE
1120—THE MAN SHE'LL MARRY
1159—IT HAPPENED ONE WEDDING
1174—MITCH TAKES A WIFE
1188—ALL I WANT FOR CHRISTMAS

Don't miss any of our special offers. Write to us at the following address for information on our newest releases.

Harlequin Reader Service
U.S.: 3010 Walden Ave., P.O. Box 1325, Buffalo, NY 14269
Canadian: P.O. Box 609, Fort Erie, Ont. L2A 5X3

GRAM'S STRAWBERRY PIE

4–5 heaping cups whole fresh strawberries
1 1/2 tbsp cornstarch or 2 tbsp tapioca
1 cup sugar
1 tbsp butter
1 baked pie crust

Pour strawberries into a medium saucepan and mash slightly. Add cornstarch and sugar. Cook until thick, about 20–30 minutes, stirring often to prevent burning. Add butter and stir until melted. Pour into baked pie crust. Cool, chill and serve with ice cream or whipped cream.

Chapter One

Standing on the floating dock, D.J. Hatcher flipped his aviator glasses atop his head. "I remember you—Liza Miller."

The way his steel-gray eyes flitted over her loose-fitting summer blouse and slacks made her wonder if he could see right through them. But the slacks were lined and the blouse wasn't see-through, so of course he couldn't.

All the same, her face grew warm. "You remembered my name." It had been nearly three years since they'd last seen each other, and she was impressed. "What a memory."

But then, it probably wasn't every day that the pilot dealt with a sobbing disaster of a passenger.

D.J. stood by the ladderlike steps to help any of the nine other passengers onto the float to climb aboard the seaplane. Not quite ready to board, Liza shaded her eyes from the late-morning Seattle sun and studied him. A good five to six inches taller than she was, D.J. wore faded jeans and a blue shirt with the sleeves rolled up. Above the shirt pocket, the blue-and-white Island Air logo. Military-short dark brown hair, strong jaw, thick wrists, broad shoulders and flat belly. Narrow hips, masculine bulge....

She adjusted her gaze and cleared her throat. "I remember you, too."

Though three years ago she'd been too distraught to appreciate what a good-looking male he was. Distraught? She'd been a basket case. Who wouldn't have been, when a few hours earlier, just before their wedding, her fiancé had announced he was in love with someone else?

Liza had never forgotten the man who'd whisked her away from Halo Island that day. After all the pain and humiliation, D.J.'s kindness and compassion had done much to soothe her raw feelings.

"So…" Hands low on his hips, he stood there, the brilliant blue June sky and glistening water of Lake Union providing the perfect backdrop. "How you doing these days?"

"Much better than the last time I saw you." Which was absolutely true. The past was behind her now, and she was almost at the point where she wanted to start dating again.

"Didn't I say you'd be okay?"

Liza smiled as she recalled that D.J. had been through his own emotional hell. He'd shared his story the same night she'd left Halo Island, telling her about his wife of less than two years running off with his best friend from college. Who also happened to be his business partner. "What about you?" she asked. "How are you?"

"Never better."

He didn't quite meet her eyes, however, making her wonder.

"Heading back to the island for a visit, huh?"

Liza nodded. "My grandmother has organized a family

reunion." Following which she was going to stay on the island to help Gram move to a retirement community—after fifty-four years in the same house. The very thought of emptying and selling the cottage where Gram and Grandpop had lived their entire married life… Well, it was going to be an emotional six weeks.

The last of the other passengers had disappeared into the plane, and D.J. glanced at his watch. "We'll be taking off soon. You'd best board."

As Liza climbed the ladder, she could feel his gaze on her. For the first time in three years she wished she'd dressed in clothes that fit a little better, instead of the shapeless things she'd taken to wearing. But if you hid your figure and stopped wearing makeup, men left you alone. And she'd wanted to be left alone.

There was only one seat left, in the back. As Liza sat and fastened her seat belt, the plane bobbed gently in the water. From here, if she stretched her neck sideways, she could see D.J. up front, busy with final preparations prior to takeoff.

He'd slipped on a headset and was fiddling with the controls, his broad shoulders straining his shirt.

Be still my heart, she thought, which was such a cliché that she had to snicker. And marvel at herself. Why this male? Why now?

She hadn't paid much attention to men in ages—not since that awful afternoon Timothy had left her stranded by the altar of the Halo Island Church. But she noticed now.

The plane's engine roared to life, then settled to a steady hum. Since there was no flight attendant, D.J. swiveled in the pilot's seat and spoke to everyone himself.

"Welcome aboard Island Air. I'm D.J. Hatcher, and I love working here." His mouth quirked. "I also own the business." Passengers laughed. He explained that Island Air also flew to Vancouver, B.C., Alaska and other places. "Please fasten your seat belts and leave them buckled," he said. Then he gave a quick rundown of the length of the flight—approximately one hour—and described their route over Puget Sound. There were no toilets on board, no food and nothing to drink. Sick sacks and briefing cards were tucked in the backs of the seats, with life vests stowed underneath. He pointed out the emergency exits, which were located on both sides of the plane.

Finished with his remarks, he turned around and began to taxi the plane.

The woman sitting across the aisle from Liza, a pretty blonde who looked about her age, turned to her and bit her lip. "I've never been on a seaplane before. I'm nervous."

"Don't be. It's a little bumpy, but the view is spectacular. And D.J.'s a terrific pilot."

"He sure is cute. I saw you talking to him." She looked envious. "Is he your boyfriend?"

"No." For the second time Liza felt her cheeks turn pink. "He's just a friend." Even though she'd only talked to him that one evening, they'd shared enough to make her consider him more than an acquaintance. "What brings you to Halo Island?"

"A former colleague of mine, actually my boss for a short time, lives here. She and her husband invited me to come visit, so I'm going over for a three-day weekend. I'm Kendra Eubanks."

She offered her hand. Liza shook it. "Liza Miller. You'll love the island."

As the plane lifted from Lake Union, Kendra glanced out. Then turned back to Liza. "So you've been to Halo Island before?"

"I was born and raised there. Maybe I know your friend. What's her name?"

"Tina Chase is her married name. She used to be Tina Morrell. When she got married and moved back here, she recommended me as her replacement. We've been friends ever since."

"I remember Tina. She was a year ahead of me in school, but we worked on the yearbook and pep squad together. I haven't seen her since she went off to college." Liza had always liked the plucky girl, who'd survived the loss of both parents and gone on to make a success of herself—thanks to the loving care of her fellow islanders. "Last I heard, she had a great job in Seattle. I had no idea she'd gotten married or moved back to the island."

"It all happened last Christmas. Do you know Ryan Chase? He has a little girl and he recently bought the Halo Island Bank. I think he moved to the island from someplace else."

"I don't recognize the name, but I haven't been back in three years." Since that horrible afternoon. The worst part of it all had been Liza's mother, who'd actually blamed *Liza* for the whole mess.

"No wonder this happened," she'd said. "If you'd quit your teaching job and moved in with Timothy, instead of forcing him to endure a long-distance relationship… I will never live this down."

Liza pushed away the painful memory. "He must've settled there after I left."

"You haven't been home in three years?" Kendra's eyebrows arched. "Wow, that's a long time."

"I've been busy." Avoiding her mother and Art, her mother's brand-new husband, who lived there. Liza had only seen them once in three years, at their wedding in Barbados the previous summer. A retired stockbroker, Art certainly had enough money for the expensive celebration. It had been a brief, awkward reunion, with Diane pretending she'd never said those awful things and Liza still smarting, although not about to pick a fight and ruin the occasion. Her own father had died fifteen years earlier, and she was happy that her mother had found another man to love. "But my grandmother, who lives on the island, has visited me often."

They called each other several times a week, too. Whereas Liza and her mother spoke only at Christmas and on birthdays, their conversations stilted and brief. Her mother had never apologized for what she'd said and Liza knew she never would. That was not Diane Julian's way.

"What do you do?" Kendra asked.

"I'm an elementary school teacher up in Bellingham." Which was ninety miles north of Seattle. She'd been teaching for six years now, two of them working as a substitute teacher for three different schools. "Or I was. I was just laid off." Again.

"I'm sorry," Kendra said.

"I'm used to it. When you don't have a continuing contract, it happens a lot."

It didn't seem to matter that Liza lived and breathed teaching and that she gave her heart and soul to the kids in her classrooms. She didn't have enough seniority to keep the same job from one year to the next, and every time she had to move on it felt like a big slap in the face. Until she had a continuing contract, there would be no job stability. And Liza wanted stability. She was tired of not knowing what would happen at the end of every school year.

"How long are you staying on the island?" Kendra asked.

"Through July." In no mood for further conversation, Liza nodded at Kendra's window. "It's a gorgeous day and you really don't want to miss the view."

When Kendra turned to look, Liza gave a quiet sigh of relief and stared out her own window. But with her life recently turned upside down, it was difficult to appreciate the sparkling water, flawless blue skies and the Cascade Mountains beyond.

Liza looked forward to being on the island again. Or would have if not for her mother. Fortunately, Diane and Art had scheduled a month-long trip to Australia, in celebration of their first anniversary. They were heading out early in July, a good week before Gram's move. Leaving Liza to shoulder the brunt of the packing and the move itself. Naturally.

But that was a month away. Liza dreaded facing her mother. Still, this visit wasn't about her, it was about her grandmother, who needed her.

And for Gram, Liza would have borne anything.

As D.J. FLEW OVER the sound on a route as familiar to him as his own hand, he thought about Liza Miller. It'd been three years since he'd seen her, but he remembered that early evening trip as if it were yesterday. Summers were always swamped with tourists flying to and from the island, but on that particular flight she'd been his only passenger. He'd been headed to Seattle, anyway, in a piston Beaver, smaller than the ten-seat turbine Otter he was flying today, to hook up with the woman he was seeing at the time. Nothing serious. Just dinner, a movie and sex.

It had turned out to be a good thing that she was the only passenger, since she'd been a real mess. Not at first glance, however. Striding down the dock toward the seaplane, she'd moved with long, rolling steps. He remembered her hip-swinging walk, made memorable by a short skirt and great legs. The snug V-neck T-shirt had been nice, too. Nothing like the modest clothing she was wearing today.

He also remembered the stricken look in her red-rimmed eyes, the wilted flowers woven into a fancy hairdo that looked as if it'd been through a windstorm. D.J. did not handle crying women well, especially when he was flying a plane. Wondering whether she was stable enough for the sometimes bumpy hour-long ride, he'd suggested she come back the next morning, when she felt better. He'd never forget her raised chin or her startling reply.

"If I stay on this island one more second, there's no telling what I might do—including strangling my mother. Get me out of here *now*."

Since she was the only passenger, he'd invited her to sit in the copilot's seat up front. She'd slid in beside him, fastened her seat belt and sat mute and stiff as he taxied along the water and then lifted off.

The plane wasn't more than two hundred feet above the sound, with a spectacular view of the sinking sun, when she broke down. D.J. had to work the flaps in order to climb to two thousand feet, but the plane did most of the work, and so he'd been able to listen to her.

"And I thought *mine* was the worst story ever," he recalled saying. Then he'd shared his sorry past, to help her realize she wasn't the only person who'd ever been made a fool of. "Imagine catching your wife in bed with your so-called best friend and business partner." Talk about harsh. D.J. knew what shock and betrayal felt like, and he had called himself lunkhead, idiot and stupid more times than he could count. "You *will* get past this."

She'd sniffled. "At the moment I'm not so sure about that."

"What do you do, workwise?"

"I'm a teacher."

"Lose yourself in your job," he'd advised. "That'll help." It had certainly helped him.

More than once he'd thought about her, wondering how she was. She looked good—not that a man could see much of her body in those clothes. With shoulder-length wavy brown hair, big green eyes and a generous mouth, she was just as pretty as he remembered. Much better, in fact, without the swollen eyes and runny nose.

No doubt she'd found some lucky guy to keep her warm at night. If D.J. had been into dating, he'd envy that boyfriend of hers. But he wasn't. With running the company and his money troubles demanding all his attention, who had time for dating? That and the fact that he did not intend to fall for any woman, ever again. Been there, done that, and it hurt like hell.

He'd lied when he'd told Liza he'd never been better. It'd been four years since Sheila and Ethan had run off together, and he was still untangling the financial mess they'd left him with. The five-year balloon payment on the loan he and Ethan had arranged when they'd bought and expanded Island Air was due the fifteenth of August, just eight short weeks away. If things had gone as planned, D.J. would have been able to save what he needed to make the payment. But life didn't always follow the path you expected. With a payroll, five planes to maintain and insure, climbing fuel bills and the mountain of debt that Sheila had run up, he'd spent every penny to keep the company and himself afloat.

D.J. didn't have the money he needed for the balloon payment. And now he was on the verge of losing the airline he loved, lived and breathed. On the verge of being a failure. At the thought of this his shoulders stiffened and his stomach knotted.

Ahead was the Strait of Juan de Fuca and the San Juan Islands. Halo Island was a thousand feet west. Time to forget his problems for a while and prepare for landing.

He adjusted the flaps, then pushed the mic button. "We're starting the descent, folks, so make sure those seat belts are fastened. After we land, please stay seated. I'll let you know when you can unbuckle."

He made his usual smooth landing, the plane's skis slicing through the water. Taxiing forward, he skimmed alongside a dock, pulled the throttle and braked to a stop. As soon as he killed the engine, he undid his own seat belt, stood and moved to the exit.

After opening and securing the door, he nodded at the passengers. "All right, you're free to leave. Hope you enjoyed the ride. Thanks for flying Island Air, and see you again."

D.J. went first. Down the steps to the float, then onto the dock. He stayed close, ready to lend a hand.

Men and women filed out, thanking him. Second to last came a busty blonde he'd noticed earlier. She gave him a hot look. Accepted his help and slipped her business card into his palm. She was exactly his type, but he was more interested in Liza Miller, who was right behind her.

He stuffed the card into his jeans pocket to throw away later and offered Liza his hand. Like the blonde, she took it. Unlike the blonde, her fingers were uncertain and cold—even though it was a warm, sunny afternoon.

Her eyes met his. They were vast and clear and green. Beautiful. They widened slightly, and he realized he'd held on to her longer than necessary.

He released his grip and gave a curt nod. "Take care."

"I will. Thanks for the ride. I…well, I appreciate everything you did for me. Before."

"No problem. Enjoy your visit."

He was sorely tempted to find out how long she'd be in town. And whether she had a boyfriend—and if not, to ask her out. Instead he watched her walk away, a suitcase in each hand and a purse slung over her shoulder.

Because what was the point of asking? He had no time for anything except saving his airline.

He didn't expect to see her again until she caught a plane back to Seattle. With seven pilots—D.J. always hired extras during tourist season—he might not see her again, period. Or, hell, maybe she'd catch a ferry to Anacortes and hop a bus back to Seattle.

He was scheduled for another round-trip flight to Seattle

an hour from now. Meantime, Joe was waiting at the Salty
Dog, a block away, to talk to him about something. The
blue-collar restaurant was home of the best fish sandwiches
in town, and D.J. was hungry enough to eat two of them.
Pushing Liza Miller from his thoughts, he strode forward.

As LIZA WALKED toward the asphalt parking lot adjacent to
the dock, she resisted the urge to turn around and see if D.J.
was watching her. For a moment there, when he'd helped
her down, she thought she'd seen a spark of interest. But
then he'd turned abrupt and businesslike, and she knew
she'd imagined any attraction.

Which was for the best, since she wasn't quite ready for
that, anyway. Especially not here on the island, close to her
mother. When she fell in love again, as she dearly hoped
someday she would, Diane would be the last to know.
Besides, with a family reunion this weekend, and then
helping Gram sort through her things and move, plus
checking the Internet for job postings (*please, please,
please,* let her find a teaching job soon), there'd be no time
for anything else.

As anxious as Liza was about the job situation, and as
filled with dread about seeing Diane, at the moment, with
the sun shining and a soft sea-scented breeze ruffling her
hair, it was hard to feel anything but a lazy warmth and con-
tentment. Above the wavelets that sparkled and danced,
pelicans, herons and gulls circled in search of fish. Liza
couldn't help smiling. Whale sightings frequently dazzled
locals and tourists. During the summers there wasn't a
more beautiful place to be than Halo Island.

She waved at a taxi idling near the dock. She hadn't told

her grandmother her exact arrival time, and needed a ride. Instead of flying, she could have driven her own car onto the ferry in Anacortes, but the combination of summer crowds and small ferries made for long wait times. If she needed to drive anyplace while she was here, she'd borrow her grandmother's car.

The cabdriver, a slim, youngish man, got out and loaded her suitcases into the trunk. "Where to?" he asked.

"Clam Digger Way." The street where Gram lived, on the opposite end of the island.

"That's a nice area. Lots of pretty houses."

He signaled and waited to turn onto Treeline Road, which ran the length of the seventeen-mile-long island. Things hadn't changed much since Liza had last been here. Summer tourists always tripled the population, and the road teemed with a steady stream of cars.

"Have you been to the island before?" the driver asked.

"Lots of times. I grew up here."

"Lucky you. My wife and I moved here last year. This is a great place to live. Everyone is so friendly."

Another motorist stopped to let them in, and at last the taxi pulled in to the traffic. Liza took advantage of the slower-than-usual drive to enjoy the beautiful leafy trees on both sides of the road. Beyond them, she caught glimpses of the houses that always had been here. At least a dozen cyclists sped by on a bike trail that wove between the road and the woods.

After three years away, it felt good to be home again. Except the island wasn't her home, not any more.

The driver glanced in the rearview mirror. "Ever heard of the band Clanking Chains?"

Liza shook her head.

"They're an up-and-coming local group and they're really good. My wife's brother's friend is their drummer. They've been playing gigs in Seattle and Portland lately, but they're at the Gull's Nest this weekend. You should go. They're on from nine to midnight."

Liza knew the pub well. "I haven't been there since college," she said. Back then, she'd spent many an evening nursing a beer and dancing and talking with friends—sometimes with Paul and Mark, her cousins, when they visited. "I'll try to make it." Depending on what Gram had planned.

At last the cab slowed and turned onto Clam Digger Way, the narrow two-lane road that paralleled the beach.

"Which house?" the driver asked.

"The third from the last."

The cab's wheels crunched over the white gravel driveway leading up to the snow-white blue-shuttered cottage, which looked as neat and well kept as always. Red and yellow roses climbed the lattice fence that bracketed the small front yard, and petunias, dahlias and sweet peas spilled from the window boxes. The house and its flowers always had been Gram's pride and joy. How was she going to give them up?

"Nice place," the driver said. "Someone has a green thumb."

"My grandmother. This is her home."

For a little while longer. A few months from now, the house would belong to someone else.

Filled with a sense of melancholy, Liza paid the driver. Hefting her suitcases, she headed up the stone walkway that her grandparents had laid themselves. Every window in front, and there were many, offered an unobstructed view of the ocean. And of the men, women and children enjoying the public beach that stood between the fenced front yard and the water.

Grandpop had left Gram with a comfortable living, but she'd always preferred to do her own gardening and cleaning, claiming she didn't want strangers tinkering with her plants or snooping about her house. Now, though, it was likely that someone else helped with the upkeep. Probably Liza's mother, who for all her faults, loved Gram as much as Liza did.

While Liza was here she intended to take over those chores, which would no doubt be a relief to Diane, who had her own yard to keep up. Art was a wealthy man. They could have hired a gardener, but Diane was like her mother that way, preferring to do her own work.

At some point today, Liza knew she'd see her mother, but for now she was focused on Gram. As she stepped onto the front stoop, her grandmother opened the screen door.

Slightly bent over, more than she had been when she'd visited Liza at Christmas, she beamed. "Hello, honey. I hoped you'd arrive before the others."

Her skin was pale and weathered, but her green eyes, which Liza had inherited, sparkled. She held out her arms and engulfed Liza in a hug that was as hearty as always.

When Liza pulled back, she managed a watery smile. "You look good, Gram."

Her grandmother dismissed the compliment with an airy wave. "I'm old." She squinted at Liza, her own eyes growing misty. "Don't cry or I will, too. Leaving my home won't be easy."

"I know." Liza wiped her eyes.

"With your mother and Art busy sorting out their vacation plans, I don't know how I'd manage without you."

"I'm happy to do whatever I can."

"That's a big comfort to me. Let's talk about something more cheerful, shall we? Your uncle Jake and cousins called a little while ago. They're stuck in a long ferry line in Anacortes, and probably won't be under way for hours. But they should be here by dinnertime. If they were smart like you, they would've flown in. But this way, I get you to myself for a little while."

Liza wondered when her mother would show up, but didn't ask. "Are they staying here, too?"

"You know your uncle Jake. He's putting himself and the rest of the family up at the Island Resort."

Which was down the beach a few miles. With all that was going on, staying someplace else probably wasn't a bad idea. Besides, Uncle Jake, who'd been divorced for ten years and was the successful owner of a tool and die-making business in Portland, enjoyed spending his money on his kids.

"Would you rather I stayed someplace else, too?" Liza asked.

If so, expensive or not, she'd find a hotel. Anything was better than staying with her mother. Though finding a room this time of year might not be easy.

"Of course not. I'm glad you're staying with me. There's so much to do between now and when I move, and with you living here, it'll be easier. Now, it's way past lunchtime, and you must be famished. I certainly am. I'll make us some sandwiches. Tuna fish all right?"

"Perfect, but you don't have to do that, Gram. Why don't I make the sandwiches."

"Because it gives me pleasure to do it myself. Go on and unpack." She glanced at Liza's clothes. "It's supposed to get hot this afternoon, so you'll want to change into something cooler. Besides, you're too young for that wrinkly old-lady blouse and pants."

Ouch. Sometimes her grandmother reminded her of her mother. Only Gram made her comments with warmth and love.

"They're linen—a classic," Liza said. "Linen is supposed to wrinkle."

"It's also supposed to fit. Those clothes are too big for you, and that beige makes you look washed out. You're so pretty, with such a nice figure. Don't you think it's time you forgot that Timothy business and moved on with your life?"

What to say? That she knew Gram was right, but she was afraid of getting hurt again? "I'm working on it," Liza said.

"That's all you can do, honey. Take your things upstairs. Then we'll eat."

Using the upstairs was a given. When Gram had been pregnant with Uncle Jake, Grandpop had converted half of the attic into a bedroom and tiny bathroom. The rest was storage. Diane's bedroom had been on the main floor, in what now was the TV room. Liza had lived up here since the age of sixteen. She'd moved in with her grandmother shortly after her father died, leaving her with no one to act as a buffer against her mother's constant criticism. Liza still slept up here whenever she visited Halo Island.

Once Gram moved, where would she stay? Liza didn't want to think about that right now.

As she crossed the cozy living room and headed upstairs, she wondered whether her grandmother wasn't right. Maybe it was time to ditch the stuffy outfits. Liza thought about D.J. Hatcher, and her unexpected attraction to him. If that wasn't a sign, what was?

When she did start dating again, it'd be with a man who lived where she lived. After what had happened with Timothy, she wasn't about to try another long-distance romance.

Gram kept the main floor painted and in good repair, but up here the braided rug and striped wallpaper were old and faded. The wood floor was dull and scratched, and the single bed creaked whenever Liza turned over. All the same, with two picture windows, one facing the sound and one overlooking the small backyard and the woods beyond, she'd never minded sleeping in the outdated room.

Potential buyers might not pay top dollar unless the upstairs looked nicer, however. Liza would strip the wallpaper and then paint the walls, she decided. And wax and buff the floor.

She hung her blouses, jeans, shorts and dresses in the closet, alongside more than a few things left from the last time she'd stayed here, the week before what was supposed to have been her wedding day.

Liza's "before" clothes included a rainbow of fuchsia, royal blue and sun yellows that complemented her skin tones and her body. Age-appropriate clothes for the twenty-eight-year-old woman she'd been. Most of them were still appropriate for thirty-one.

Next to those outfits, the items she'd brought with her today, in various tones of beige or white, looked—as her grandmother had so bluntly put it—like old-lady clothes.

A critical glance at her reflection in the full-length mirror on the closet door confirmed Gram's opinion. Her blouse and slacks completely hid her figure, which had been the point.

It certainly had worked well today.

She pulled out a fitted scooped-neck hot-pink blouse and a pleated white-and-pink-striped miniskirt and held them in front of her. Would D.J. Hatcher have asked her for a date if she'd been wearing this outfit instead?

Rolling her eyes at the question, she returned the blouse and skirt to the closet. "Why am I even thinking about him?"

For all she knew, he was happily involved with some beautiful woman.

Mindful of her grandmother's comments, but still not quite ready for bright colors or snug-fitting clothes, she changed into shorts and a roomy cream-colored T-shirt. Washed up in the bathroom, then headed downstairs.

Chapter Two

The Salty Dog smelled of grilled fish and fries, making D.J.'s mouth water. As usual, the place was packed. Yet the minute he was inside the air-conditioned diner, he spotted Joe Hawlings. In a booth at the back, with his arm around Brianna Simpson, the hot little blonde he'd dated for the past month.

She wasn't as hot as Liza Miller. Surprised by this thought, D.J. frowned as he approached the two. There'd been nothing sexy about those clothes. Yeah, but those big, green eyes, that smile. And the hint of womanly curves that no clothing could hide....

"Hey there, Joe. Brianna." He spoke loudly to be heard over the noise, slid into the booth and eyed his friend's companion. "How'd the tour go?"

Brianna sang with the Clanking Chains, a local band that everyone thought was going places. The past two weeks she and the rest of the group had been playing Portland and Seattle. This weekend they were home for a gig, but next week they'd be off again.

"We're drawing good crowds and great reviews. But I

missed the big guy here." She smiled at Joe, whose eyes went soft. "It's good to be back for a few days."

Looking relaxed and in love—for the moment, anyway—Joe pulled her closer to his side. "I'm sure happy you're here."

A pilot with Island Air, Joe was off today, just as he was every Friday. D.J.'s day off was Saturday. He hated the fact that he couldn't fly seven days a week, but a pilot was allowed only thirty-four hours of flight time per week and was required to take off a minimum one day out of every seven, as well.

D.J. signaled to Wanda, the waitress who'd worked here since long before he'd moved to town. Dressed in a pink uniform, and with pencil and order pad in hand, she hurried over. "What'll you have, sugar?"

She was exactly his kind of woman—fun-loving, and jaded on the subject of marriage. But she was in her late forties. D.J. was thirty-five, and he wasn't attracted to her. They were simply friends.

"Iced coffee, two salmon burgers and fries," he said.

Joe nodded. "I'll have the same."

Brianna smiled at Wanda. "I'd like a diet soda and a crab salad, with the dressing on the side."

"Coming up." As busy as the restaurant was, Wanda moved away at a fast clip.

"How's the flying today?" Joe asked.

"Same as yesterday—busy." D.J. settled back and crossed his arms. "But you didn't invite me here to talk about that. What's up?"

Joe glanced at Brianna. "You tell him."

"Okay. You know the band is singing tonight at the Gull's Nest."

"Right. I'll be there."

"This friend of mine, Kiki, is visiting from Missoula." Where Brianna was from. "Or will be, once she gets off the ferry this afternoon. She's really cute, and she'll be here all weekend. Joe and I would like you to sit with her tonight, while I'm singing."

That didn't sound half bad, but the way they both eyed D.J. made him wonder. "What's the catch?"

"Catch?" Brianna repeated. She and Joe shared a long look. Then she stood. "I'm going to the ladies' room to wash my hands. I'll let Joe explain."

Joe watched his woman saunter off, then leaned his forearms on the table. "It's like this. If you're not around, Kiki will be hanging on to Brianna and me like an extra seaplane ski. Brianna's been gone two long weeks. We haven't been alone in a while, if you get my meaning, and with Kiki arriving in less than an hour... We're hoping you'll entertain her after the gig tonight, so we can have some quality time alone."

"I have an early morning meeting Saturday with our accountant," D.J. said. "I wasn't planning on a late night. Besides, what if I don't like her?"

"I'm not asking you to sleep with her—just keep her busy for a few hours. Come on, Deej, I'm dyin' here. I'd do the same for you, I swear."

While Wanda delivered the drinks, D.J. mulled things over. It'd been a long time since he'd wanted a woman the way Joe wanted Brianna, but he understood. If entertaining Kiki for a few hours meant losing a little sleep, well,

God knew his accountant, Carter Boyle, had seen him at his worst more than once.

As soon as Wanda hurried off again, he shrugged. "Okay, I'll do it."

WHEN LIZA ENTERED the kitchen, her grandmother was sitting on one of the padded banquettes in the breakfast nook, looking out at the water. Anyone on the beach could have turned around and looked through the wraparound bay windows, but with the house a good hundred yards from the beach, they probably couldn't see much.

Sitting at the place that had been set for her, Liza licked her lips. "I've always loved your tuna salad. Yum."

She bit eagerly into her sandwich, and her grandmother did the same.

"If you don't mind my asking, who's looking after your apartment while you're here?" Gram said.

"Bill and Noreen, two of my teacher friends. They're building a house and they needed a place to stay for the rest of the month. So the timing works out great for both them and me." Their paying part of the rent helped, too. "If all goes well, soon after I head back to Bellingham I'll be moving to a different city for a new teaching job." Under the table Liza crossed her fingers.

"Are you at all worried about finding another school?"

Applying and interviewing always were stressful. So was moving to a new community. Add to that the fact that she might not even *find* a job...but Liza wasn't about to share her anxieties. "I've done it lots of times, so I'm used to it. School districts will start posting their openings soon, and while I'm here I'll be checking the Internet every day."

"That sounds like a smart plan. Any school would be lucky to have you."

"Thanks, Gram. I think so, too."

In comfortable silence they returned to their lunch.

"You know, the upstairs could use a face-lift," Liza said in between bites. "I thought that while I'm here, I might as well fix it up. If that's okay with you."

"If you want to tackle that job, I'm all for it."

"Great. After the rest of the family leaves, I'll stop at the hardware store and pick up some color swatches for you."

"Any color is fine with me. You decide."

That her grandmother didn't care about something as important as the color of the upstairs only emphasized the fact that she was loosening her ties to the house.

"Are you positive you want to move to that retirement community?" Liza asked. "You've lived here forever, and downsizing to a tiny apartment… Well, that'll be a big adjustment."

"You're right, I've been here since God invented dirt." Her grandmother's eyes twinkled. "But the house really is too much for me now. It's time to leave."

Her teasing look surprised Liza. "I'm confused. A little while ago, you were teary-eyed about moving. Now you seem almost happy."

"Sometimes I *do* feel sad, but most of the time I'm okay. I've thought about it for a long time and I'm ready to make the change." She reached across the table to pat Liza's hand. "Sunset Manor is a beautiful retirement community. Even your mother thinks so, and you know how persnickety she is. It's in a great location, too, across the street from Halo Island Park. I've planned a picnic lunch at the park tomorrow, after I show you and the others my apartment there. They're still making it pretty with new flooring, fixtures and paint, but you'll be able to see it. Once you do, I know you'll feel better about this move."

If what Gram said was true and her picky mother liked the place, then it must be all right. Liza figured she'd find out soon enough.

"Then, after the picnic, I'll be making an important announcement." Gram's face gave away nothing.

"That sounds serious." Was she sick? She *did* look a bit pale. Liza couldn't even pretend to smile. "Can't you tell me now?"

"That wouldn't be fair to everyone else. Now, wait till you hear what Mr. Tillitsen down the road did last week."

Neatly changing the subject, Gram launched into a story about her neighbor's garden adventures with various birds, rabbits and deer. Which was entertaining and came with a point—the subject was closed until after the picnic tomorrow.

Liza was worried, and while she and her grandmother chatted easily she studied the older woman for signs of poor health. Other than a paler-than-usual complexion, she saw none, but then she was no doctor.

When they finished, Gram set down her napkin and gave Liza an apologetic look. "You should know that while you unpacked, I called your mother. She'll be here shortly. I thought you two should talk before Art and everyone else arrives."

Liza groaned. "I suppose it's time to face her. But I dread it."

"Well, don't. It's time you two mended fences."

"I'm not sure that's possible."

"Life is short, Liza, and you only get one mother."

"That goes both ways. She said some pretty mean things to me." No need to clarify *when*—on Liza's aborted wedding day.

"She was upset, honey, and so were you. Everyone was."

"Yes, but you and the rest of the family were on *my* side." Liza grimaced. "Mother owes *me* an apology."

"You're absolutely right." Gram sighed and suddenly looked tired. "But Diane is stubborn, just as your grandpop was. She's not likely to change. You'll have to take the first step."

"It's always that way, and I'm tired of it."

"Do it for me, honey. And for the two of you. Your mother and Art are so happy, and I know she'd like to sort things out with you."

Not at all certain she believed that but wanting to please her grandmother, Liza gave in. "Oh, all right."

She heard the screen door swing open and slap shut, and Diane's familiar no-nonsense tread on the oak floor.

Then her mother was there, hesitating briefly in the doorway between the kitchen and the dining room.

Shoulders squared, she headed for the breakfast nook, her coral lips forming a smile as artificial as her honey-blond hair. "Hello, Liza."

Too tense even to fake a reciprocal smile, Liza shifted in her seat. "Mother."

Trim, stylishly dressed and carefully groomed, Diane kissed her mother's proffered cheek, then sat down beside Liza, trapping her between herself and the wall.

"I would have been here earlier, only I had a garden club meeting."

Her gaze drifted over Liza, and if her forehead hadn't been Botoxed into smoothness, tiny lines of disapproval would no doubt have formed. Probably she didn't like the T-shirt. Liza raised her chin.

"Well." Gram slid across the bench she was seated on. She stood and stacked the sandwich plates. "I believe I'll take a nap before the rest of the family arrive. We're eating out back on the patio, by the way, so one of you should set up the picnic table and clean the grill."

"I will," Liza said. "I'll take care of the dishes, too, so leave them in the sink." *Stay,* she tried to telegraph with her eyes, but Gram wasn't looking her way.

Neither she nor her mother spoke until her grandmother left the kitchen, but the tension between them said plenty. Liza's mother was every bit as uncomfortable as she was.

"How was your flight?" she asked, folding her manicured hands on the surface of the maple table.

"Fine." *I have a crush on the pilot, but I'll never tell you about it.*

"Your grandmother told me you lost your job, and that you'll probably be moving again. That's got to be hard."

"I'll survive." Before her mother could comment, Liza changed the subject. "Do you really like the retirement community she's moving into?"

"Her apartment there is very nice—or at least it will be, when they finish the renovations. Even so, I can't quite picture my mother living anyplace other than this house. It's going to be a hard few weeks. And with Art and me so busy, getting ready for Australia…" Diane bit her lip. "Your being here to help makes it easier."

"Thanks. She's always been so generous to me. This is my chance to pay her back a little."

"I'm going to help, too, as much as I can. If Art and I had known that Mother planned to move this summer, we'd have postponed our trip until fall. But she didn't tell us until a few months ago."

They probably still could change their plans, but Liza wanted her mother gone, so she said nothing. "We'll manage just fine," she said, smoothing her T-shirt.

Diane's mouth curled downward. "That shirt isn't at all flattering. Two adorable boutiques have opened since you were last here. Why don't I take you shopping."

Gram had criticized her clothes, too, but coming from Diane… Liza bristled under the criticism. "I don't need or want anything from you, Mother."

It was Diane's turn to stiffen. "Suit yourself. But let me know if you change your mind. You know, now that you've been laid off, you could go back to school and get an advanced degree. Then you could become a principal."

It was an old bone of contention. To her ears, "My daughter is a principal," sounded better than, "She teaches elementary school."

Diane never had understood and never would, but once again Liza tried to explain. "As I've said a dozen times before, I don't want to be an administrator. I love teaching, and if I ever do go back for another degree, it'll be geared toward that. Understood?"

Her mother sighed, then nodded. "But as a teacher, you don't have job security."

"I will when I finally get a continuing contract."

"*If* you get one. And speaking of job security, you should

have told me about losing your job. Instead, I heard about it from your grandmother." Diane sniffed and looked hurt.

The nerve! "So you could say something mean?" *And make me feel even worse?* "No, thank you."

Her mother recoiled, which should have given Liza some satisfaction. But it didn't. She blew out a breath. "You're right, I should've told you—but I've been too angry. Am I ever going to get an apology?"

Her mother stared at the table before replying. "Believe me, if I could take back what I said that day… Well, I can't. But it's been three years. I'm married and I've begun a new and wonderful phase of my life, and I'd like to put all the bad memories behind us and start fresh."

It was as close to *I'm sorry* as Liza would ever get, she knew. And she really did want to get along with her mother. Skeptically, she nodded. "I'll try."

This was good enough for Diane. The tension eased from her shoulders, and she looked relieved.

"Gram said something about an announcement after lunch tomorrow. Something she doesn't want to talk about until we're all together," Liza said. "Do you know what that's about? She's not sick, is she?"

"Not that I know of. Your grandmother always had a flare for drama." A flare Diane had inherited. "I'm sure it's nothing. Listen, Liza, I'd like you to have dinner with Art and me next week. We'll go to Harvey's." The most upscale restaurant on the small island.

"All right," Liza said, already dreading the evening. "Or we could eat at Gram's. I'll cook."

"If you'd rather do that, fine." Her mother offered a brief smile. "I'm happy that we talked, Liza. I've—"

"Anybody home?" a voice boomed out. Liza's uncle Jake.

"We're here!" chimed Annabel and Wilson, her cousin Mark and his wife, Charlene's, four-year-old twins. Their footsteps pattered across the floor.

With the exception of Diane's husband Art, the rest of the family had arrived.

SEATED AT THE HEAD of the backyard picnic table, with birds chirping in the trees, Gram licked melted chocolate from her fingers. "I do love s'mores."

"Me, too," said Liza's uncle Jake, who sat to her left and was busy devouring his second one.

After a feast of barbecued chicken, potato salad and grilled vegetables, Liza was full and content. She was seated between her cousins, Paul and Mark, with her mother, Art and Mark's wife across the table. The twins were chasing each other happily around the backyard in gales of laughter.

Though Liza and her cousins talked and e-mailed each other often, she hadn't seen them in a while. This was family at its best, and these were memories to cherish. Bittersweet memories, however, in that this would be the last all-family dinner in Gram's backyard. For tomorrow night's evening meal, they'd made plans to eat out, and Sunday afternoon Uncle Jake and the cousins were leaving. A short but enjoyable reunion.

"Since we're all here, couldn't you share your news now?" Liza asked. She'd told her uncle and cousins about Gram's forthcoming announcement, and they'd speculated as to what it could be. Illness? A secret romance? Was she planning a trip? They had no clue.

Gram shook her head. "After you see my apartment and after the picnic."

"Can't you get her to talk now?" Art asked Diane. The compact but powerfully built gray-haired man liked his recently acquired family, and it was obvious that he felt comfortable here.

"She can try, but I won't say a word until tomorrow." Gram put her finger over her mouth.

Jake turned to Art, his lips twitching. "She means that, too."

Liza and her cousins looked at each other and shrugged. Want to or not, they'd have to wait.

At eight o'clock it was still daylight, a perk of living in the Pacific Northwest. But as the sun slipped toward the horizon, the air began to cool.

Still wearing shorts and a T-shirt, Liza chafed her arms. "As much fun as this is, I'm chilly. Why don't we move inside?"

"No, no, no." Little chin high and hands on her hips, Annabel shook her head. "I'm not cold, I'm sweaty hot! I want to stay out here."

"Yeah," Wilson agreed.

"No wonder you're hot." Charlene smiled at her children. "You've been running around the backyard the past half hour. You both need showers and it's almost bedtime. We should get back to the resort."

"Do we have to?"

"I'm not tired."

The twins protested at the same moment.

"And I'm not ready for you to go just yet," Gram said. "This reunion is so short. Why don't you big kids spend some time together. Go out and have some fun. The twins can shower here, and we'll all go to bed when we're tired. They can sleep on the daybed in Diane's old room. When you get tired of visiting, you can pick them up."

"Can we stay?" Wilson said.

"Please, oh, please?" Annabel clutched her hands together eagerly.

With their soulful brown eyes and sweet faces, they were hard to resist. Liza let out a wistful sigh. Someday she hoped to have children of her own. Not until she met the right man, of course. Which she wouldn't unless she started dating again.

Dating. At the thought of it, her heart contracted. But her attraction to D.J. told her that she was ready. It was time to get back into the game, and once she was relocated, she'd begin to seek out available men.

"I'll stay here with you, Mom," Jake said. "Diane, why don't you and Art stay, too? It'll be fun."

Liza's mother, who adored the twins and was in an unusually mellow mood, glanced at Art.

He shrugged good-naturedly. "If you want to, princess, why not?"

Princess. If ever there was a nickname to fit Liza's mother, that was it.

"All right, then. Thank you all." Charlene linked her arm through Mark's. "Where shall we go?"

"The Gull's Nest," Liza said, remembering her conversation with the cabdriver. "The group that's performing tonight, the Clanking Chains, is supposed to be good." She could hardly wait to kick up her heels and dance with her cousins.

"Never heard of them." Mark gave his wife a questioning look. Charlene shook her head.

Paul looked thoughtful. "I think they played in Portland recently. Even if the band stinks, I say we go. Lots of pretty women at the Gull's Nest." He winked. "Only thing is, it's tourist season. The place will be packed."

"That's okay by Mark and me," Charlene said. "We haven't been dancing in ages. What time do you think they start?"

"The cabdriver who told me about the band said nine." Liza checked her watch. "That's in forty-five minutes." She glanced at her cousins, who were dressed in jeans and summer shirts, and decided to exchange her T-shirt and shorts for more suitable clothes.

"Let me change first," she said, avoiding her mother's knowing look. "I'll just be a minute."

Chapter Three

Seated at a table for four, D.J. sipped his draft beer while a mixture of sounds—an oldies song from the jukebox, conversation and laughter—eddied around him. An hour before the band started, the Gull's Nest was half-empty, which was fine by him.

He knew a handful of locals here tonight, and he figured the rest were tourists. Beside him, an apple-cheeked Kiki scanned the surroundings, obviously impressed with the fishermen's nets across the ceiling and the plastic replicas of gulls and fish mounted on the walls.

"This is an awesome place," she said.

D.J. guessed it was, especially for someone who'd barely set foot outside Montana. According to Kiki, she'd once traveled to Washington, D.C., with her senior high-school class, but that was it.

Brianna was right, her friend was cute. But way too young and perky for D.J. If the bouncer hadn't checked her ID, he'd have guessed she was about seventeen. She was twenty-two, the same age as Brianna, but she seemed so green that D.J. felt decades older. He did have a few years on her. She was still in school, studying to be a vet. D.J. had been out of school a while now, and had been around the block more times than he could count. In his mind, she'd have been better off with one of the college boys at the next table over.

Kiki seemed to think so, too. She kept glancing at a curly-haired male sitting there, who looked as fresh-faced as she was.

Brianna, however, was happy at this table with her man. She sat so close to Joe that she was nearly on his lap. Joe couldn't take his eyes or his hands off her, and the goofy smile on his face was something else. D.J. had never seen a man so whipped. He didn't go in for public affection, but Joe and Brianna did.

After one too many of their hot kisses, he muttered, "Get a room." But since it was almost time for Brianna's band to start playing, that wasn't going to happen for hours.

Kiki was fiddling with her shoulder-length brown hair and looking uncomfortable and D.J. figured somebody should say something, just to take the edge off. Apparently, it wouldn't be Kiki, and with Joe and Brianna lost in their own world conversation was up to him.

"More beer?" he asked.

Kiki nodded. "That'd be good."

"Hit me, too." Joe let go of Brianna, to push his mug toward D.J.

"None for me, thanks," Brianna said. She was sipping plain water until after her gig.

As D.J. emptied the last of a pitcher into their mugs he searched for something to talk about. He wished the band would start now and get things rolling, because then he wouldn't have to say a word. But it wasn't time yet.

"What do you do for fun in Missoula?" he asked.

"Well, this summer I'm interning on a ranch. Taking care of the horses and cows is fun."

"Sounds like a load of laughs."

Across the room, two women closer to D.J.'s age sipped wine. One of them, a pretty redhead, caught his eye. She smiled and gave him a heavy-lidded "I'm available" look, and he knew he could get lucky if he wanted. But he didn't, not with the redhead.

There were plenty of other attractive women here, but for some reason no one interested him. Meanwhile, Kiki kept glancing at Curly Hair whenever she thought D.J. wasn't looking. Neither of them wanted to be with the other. What a pair they were.

At eight-thirty, after giving Joe a long, juicy, embarrassing kiss, Brianna went backstage with the rest of the band. Whistling, Joe headed for the men's room.

"Looks like a nice guy over there," D.J. said, nodding at Curly Hair. "Why don't you go talk to him."

Shy, Kiki ducked her head. "I can't do that," she said, not even pretending she didn't know what he meant.

Okay. D.J. figured it was up to him to fix up the two kids. "We're out of beer. I'll get a fresh pitcher and some popcorn."

While Kiki was busy watching the band members set up, D.J. headed straight for Curly Hair. The kid's eyes about bugged out of his head.

"Easy," D.J. said. "Just wanted you to know, she's not with me. Feel free to make your move."

"Thanks, man."

By the time D.J. brought a new pitcher and some popcorn back to the table, Kiki was sitting with the college boys. She raised her eyebrows at D.J., and he nodded that he was cool with things.

Seconds later, Joe was back. "You got rid of Kiki," he said, grabbing a handful of popcorn. "Didn't you like her?"

"Maybe if I was ten years younger, I would. She's where she should be, having fun with a guy her own age."

"Well, you tried. Thanks, man."

D.J. shrugged. "It worked out great. This way she's busy for the evening. If things go well for her, you and Brianna should get that alone time you need."

D.J. and Joe were enjoying the beer and some easy conversation. But Kiki and her table were starting to get loud and raucous. No doubt drinking too much, too fast. Not D.J.'s problem, but he hoped Kiki knew what she was doing. He was waiting for the band to start, when the door opened and a new crowd spilled in.

To his surprise, Liza was at the back of the group. She was with three other people, two of them obviously a couple. Was the other guy her boyfriend?

As D.J. checked them out, he told himself he was only mildly curious. They were grinning and talking to each other like a matched set. He actually felt jealous. As if he had any right. He scratched the back of his neck. What was his problem? Hell, he wasn't even interested in Liza. But he looked, all the same.

She'd changed into jeans and a sleeveless blouse. Nothing tight, but enough that he could see the shape of her round breasts. The jeans hugged her hips and hinted at her fine legs.

Well, now. Forgetting she wasn't his type, he watched her saunter forward, even craned his neck when someone blocked his view.

Joe followed his gaze. "Who's that?"

"Her name's Liza Miller," D.J. said, looking away to sip his beer. "She used to live here. I flew her in from Seattle this afternoon."

"Sweet," Joe said. "Don't look now, but here she comes."

Sure enough, she was headed toward their table, laughing it up with her boyfriend. Her smile turned her from pretty to unbelievably beautiful. D.J. sucked in a breath. He couldn't look away.

She must have felt his stare, for suddenly she looked directly at him. The dazzling smile slipped, her eyes widened and she stumbled on something. Her boyfriend caught her arm and they kept on walking. Straight to D.J.'s table.

"Hello," she said, for some reason blushing.

"Hey, there." He nodded. "What brings you here?"

"I came to hear the band. These are my cousins. Paul, Mark and Charlene."

So the single guy was a *cousin.* Tension that D.J. hadn't realized he was harboring faded. He stood and shook hands with everyone. Then he nodded at Joe. "That's Joe Hawlings."

Joe stood, too, and also shook hands.

"D.J.'s a pilot and the owner of Island Air," Liza said. "He flew me in today."

When her cousins gave him respectful looks his chest puffed up, and he felt proud despite the company's miserable financial shape. Not even Joe knew about that. D.J. renewed his vow to somehow save the business.

"I'm a pilot with the company, too," Joe said, looking equally proud. "And my girlfriend sings with the Clanking Chains."

"Cool," Mark said. "Do you know if they're planning to come to Arizona?"

"Is that where you're from?" D.J. asked.

"Tucson. Paul lives in Portland."

On cue, Brianna and the rest of the band bounded on stage.

"We'd better sit down," Liza said.

"Where?" Mark gestured at the room. "All the tables are taken."

"Sit with us," Joe said. "We'll make room."

D.J. wasn't sure that was a good idea. Liza didn't look all that excited, either.

But Mark and Paul already were dragging over extra chairs from another table.

Too late now.

D.J. WAS THE LAST person Liza had expected to see tonight. Yet not only was he here, she was squeezed in at his table, sitting beside him.

So much for a special evening with her cousins. Mark and Charlene didn't seem to mind, but then it wasn't often they enjoyed an evening away from the twins. Paul seemed happy, too, nodding his head to the music and checking out the women.

Liza was too aware of the man beside her to relax. With six of them crowded around a table for four, she and D.J. were close enough that from time to time his thigh brushed against hers. Every time it happened, her whole body tensed as it hadn't for a long time. These were sexual feelings, and she wasn't ready for them, so she worked at keeping a distance between herself and D.J.

Wondering if he felt anything, she glanced at him from under lowered lashes. And caught him staring at her.

"What?" she said over the music.

"How's the family reunion going?" he asked in a loud voice.

"It's been great so far."

He leaned toward her, his shoulder bumping hers. "How long are you all here for?"

He was so close, she smelled the beer on his breath and his spicy aftershave. Warmth flooded her, unwelcome and daunting. She moved back a hair.

"They're leaving Sunday. I'm here through July. My gram… Well, she's getting ready to move into a retirement community and put her home on the market. I'm going to help her close up the house and move. She's lived there a long time, and the whole thing makes me sad."

Liza wasn't sure why she'd shared this with D.J. His understanding look surprised her.

"I know how you feel. A few years back, after my grandpa died, my grandma did the same thing. She didn't want to live in that big old house by herself. But she's made some great friends at her retirement community— she even has a boyfriend. Last time I talked to her, she was having a blast."

"Really? My grandmother doesn't want a boyfriend, but I'm glad to hear about the friends and the fun. That makes me feel better about the move. Thanks for easing my mind, D.J."

"Happy to help."

For a moment he was quiet, moving in his seat to the music. Then, he leaned close again.

"As I recall, you and your mom weren't getting along. Are things better now?"

He remembered that? The man seemed to have a mind like a steel trap. "Not great, but better. She got married last year, to a retired stockbroker. Her new husband takes up a lot of her time."

"Do you like him?"

"He's nice, and he makes her happy."

D.J. nodded. Sat back and stroked his chin. "I'm guessing that's why your boyfriend didn't come with you, because of your mom."

"What boyfriend? At the moment, I'm not dating."

"Huh. I just figured you were."

The song ended, but Liza barely noticed.

The way D.J. looked at her, as if *he* wanted to date her, both excited and scared her. She swallowed. "What about you? Do you have a girlfriend?"

"Girlfriends always want to get serious, and I don't do serious." The band started again, a toe-tapping song that had couples heading for the dance floor. "Want to dance?"

Did she? More important, *should* she? While Liza thought about that, Mark tugged Charlene forward. Paul headed for a nearby table and asked a woman there to dance. One elbow on the table and his head on his fist, Joe stared dreamily at his girlfriend, a sexy woman with a great bluesy voice.

"This is one of my favorite songs." D.J. shot Liza an impatient look. "You gonna dance with me or not?"

"Okay," Liza heard herself say. It was a fast song, so nothing would happen anyway.

D.J. took her hand and pulled her up. His gaze flitted over her and she was glad she'd changed. He led her past Charlene and Mark, who grinned.

Inside the sea of couples they found a tiny space and started dancing. For a big man, D.J. was amazingly limber and fluid, with a great sense of rhythm. In a black Island Air T-shirt and snug-fitting jeans, he reminded her of Patrick Swayze in *Dirty Dancing*. Not the face or hair, so much, but the hard, excellent body. Only they weren't dancing "dirty."

Liza didn't even know how to dance that way. Although, at the moment she wished she did.

D.J.'s smile warmed her, and so did his eyes. She liked the way he looked at her. The instant she formed the thought, awareness sobered his face. A heat she hadn't felt in a long time started low in her belly, and spread through her.

Startled, she glanced away. And saw Tina Morrell—no, it was Chase now, right? Looking radiantly happy. She was with a tall, attractive man who must be her husband. Kendra, the blond woman from the plane, was here, too, dancing with someone Liza didn't recognize.

Tina looked surprised to see Liza, but then grinned and waved at both her and D.J. He nodded back. Tina was too far away and it was too noisy for conversation, but Liza pantomimed calling her. Tina nodded.

Kendra glanced at D.J. Then gave Liza a narrowed-eyed knowing look and a wry smile. She probably thought Liza had lied about their being just friends.

Even the cabdriver was here, dancing with a petite woman who must be his wife. He caught sight of Liza, beamed and pointed with pride to the drummer. She gave him a thumbs-up before returning her focus to dancing.

The song ended with barely a pause. When the band broke into a slow song, D.J. pulled her into his arms. Against her better judgment she slid against him.

She was tall enough so that her head fit under his chin. It had been a long time since a man had held her, and D.J.'s arms around her felt wonderful. Liza closed her eyes and let the pulse of the music and the physical sensations wash over her. The solid feel of his body, the smell of aftershave and man.

He made a low sound she didn't understand. She pulled back to look at him. His gaze was dark and intent, and his mouth flirted with a sexy grin.

"Hey, there," he said, running his thumb across her cheek.

The touch felt both intimate and possessive. Liza forgot about the band, her cousins and everyone else. She didn't think about how scared she was or about pulling away. What she wanted was…*more.*

Her gaze locked on D.J.'s, she leaned into his hand. Cupping her face, he tipped up her chin and gave her a smoldering look. Her lips parted on a needy sigh. Hardly aware of her actions, she wrapped her arms around his neck and waited for him to kiss her.

With a heavy-lidded gaze he lowered his head. Every cell in Liza's body stretched toward him. Her eyelids fluttered shut and her mouth tingled in expectation.

Then, from some unwanted place, she heard a woman's voice.

"D.J." She sounded distressed.

D.J. did not kiss Liza. He stopped dancing. Tensed, and loosened his hold on her.

Opening her eyes, Liza saw the woman who belonged to the voice. An attractive young brunette she'd never seen before was clutching his arm and looking ready to cry.

Judging by the miserable expression on her face and the way she clung to D.J., she knew him well. And did not like him dancing with Liza.

Oh, God, he has a girlfriend.

After he'd said he didn't. Liza stepped back. Never mind that D.J. had been alone earlier in the evening. This woman must've just arrived.

Having a girlfriend and lying about it hadn't stopped him from treating Liza as if he wanted her. He was no different than Timothy. The bum.

Ignoring D.J., Liza mustered an apologetic smile for his female friend. "He didn't tell me about you. It was just a dance. No harm meant."

Before either D.J. or the other woman said a word, she spun away and pushed through the crowd.

WHAT HAD JUST HAPPENED? Confused, D.J. watched Liza bolt from the dance floor.

One minute he'd been sitting at the table, happy to have gotten rid of Kiki. The next he was on the dance floor with Liza Miller, all hot and bothered. So turned on that he'd been about to kiss her in front of a roomful of people, some of them local gossips. The island was like any small town—everyone knew everyone else's business. Not only that, but people seemed to think that a man who'd been single all this time ought to find a woman and settle down.

Which was why D.J. kept his personal stuff private.

Until tonight. He'd never had this happen before—forgotten himself and where he was. Holding Liza had felt so damn good. And when she'd looked up at him with that soft light in her eyes and her mouth so kissable, his body had gone on red alert. He was lucky he didn't have a hard-on, though he'd been halfway there.

He must be out of his mind.

Judging by what had just happened, Liza apparently thought so.

He'd been so certain she wanted him to kiss her…and maybe more. But the dirty look she'd thrown him before hurrying away made him feel about two inches tall.

And the hell of it was, he didn't even know what he'd done wrong.

He started after her—or tried to. Kiki had a viselike grip on him. Frowning, he peeled off her fingers. "What's with you?"

She gave him a bleary smile and he realized she was drunk. "That college guy turned out to be a jerk. Can I hang out with you again?"

This was why she'd interrupted the most intense dance of his life? On the other hand, he owed her for saving him from doing something he'd regret later on.

"Why not," he muttered. "But first, I need to find Liza." And apologize. Or something.

"She's your girlfriend, isn't she?" Kiki looked hurt. "You should've told me."

"I don't have one and I don't want one," D.J. said. "I'll be back."

With so many people on the dance floor, it took him a while to reach the table. Liza wasn't there. No sign of her at the bar. He asked a woman to check the bathroom. She wasn't in there, either.

D.J. rubbed a hand over his face. She'd come in with her cousins. He caught sight of two of them on the dance floor. Surely she wouldn't leave on her own. Maybe she needed some air. He sure as hell did. He strode out of the building, into the night.

Even through the thick walls of the Gull's Nest he still heard the band. They were great, with a beat no one could resist. Maybe it was the music that had him acting like a crazed man.

The night air was cool, and D.J. sucked in a deep breath. He circled the building, then checked the parking lot and the shadows cast by the streetlights. Feeling worse by the minute, he shoved his hands in his jeans pockets and trudged across the street, heading toward the nearby shops that stayed open late for tourists.

At last he spotted her half a block away, walking toward the Ice Creamery. Lengthening his stride, he quickly caught up.

"Hey, there," he said, his tone sounding gruff to his own ears.

"D.J." Her eyes widened and she stopped in the middle of the sidewalk. People were trying to pass them, so she moved onto the grass. "Haven't you caused enough trouble for one night?"

Trouble? Confused, he frowned. "Why did you take off like that?"

If looks could destroy, hers would have cut him to the bone. She raised her head like royalty and even though he stood a good half foot taller, managed to look down at him.

"Because you have a girlfriend, and she was upset by our dance. As she had every right to be."

"Girlfriend? You mean Kiki?" That Liza thought she was his girl was so outrageous he just laughed and shook his head. "She's a kid, a friend of Brianna's—Joe's lady, the singer for Clanking Chains. She's visiting for the weekend, and we only met tonight. Before you got here, she hooked up with a guy closer to her age. He turned out to be a jerk and she's plastered, so she interrupted us to ask if she could hang out with me. I said I had to find you first."

He looked Liza straight in the eye, so she'd know he was telling the truth. "There's nothing between her and me, I swear."

But damned if there wasn't already something between him and Liza.

She blinked. "Oh."

The self-righteous expression faded from her face, and her chin dropped a fraction. Yes, she believed him. A giant weight rolled off his shoulders, and he relaxed.

"I guess I'm still a little sensitive," she said. "I'm so embarrassed."

She smoothed her blouse over her hips. Her round, very sexy hips. Damned if he didn't want to pull her close and get back to what they'd started on the dance floor.

No way, he warned himself and backed up a step. He had enough on his plate. He did not want to get involved with Liza Miller.

"Hey, I understand. You were badly burned and you don't trust guys. That's exactly why I don't get serious. Men and women can't trust each other, and if they do, somebody gets hurt."

"Something we both understand," she said.

Things were okay now. He could go back to the Gull's Nest. Then she looked at him. She was just as attracted to him as he was to her—he saw it in her eyes. His body responded—a certain part of him in particular.

If she knew what was happening with Island Air, she sure as hell wouldn't be looking at you like that.

The thought cooled him down faster than a bucket of ice water. Which was a good thing. He didn't need this. Nodding at the Ice Creamery, he said, "This is a great place for ice-cream cones. You want one?"

She shook her head—a big relief. "No, thanks. I think I'll find my cousins and go home now. Good night."

"See ya," he said, even though he figured he wouldn't.

Chapter Four

Liza didn't draw in a normal breath until Mark maneuvered his rented minivan out of the crowded Gull's Nest parking lot. As he headed down dark Treeline Road, she closed her eyes and let her head fall against the headrest.

Paul was in the backseat beside her, and even though her eyes were shut she was aware of his scrutiny.

"One minute you were dancing, and the next you walked out," he said. "That guy follows you, then you come back alone and say you want to leave. What happened?"

How could Liza possibly explain, when she didn't understand herself? The strong attraction seemed to arc between the two of them on the dance floor, causing a deep ache inside her body that she didn't like or want. But it had been such a long time since she'd been with a man, and the sudden glut of sensations combined with the sensual pulse of the music had broken down her resistance. Throw in D.J.'s heated, hungry expression, and it was a wonder she could think at all.

Then finding out that Kiki wasn't his girlfriend, after all…. Liza's relief had been too strong. She didn't care one bit for her intense feelings for D.J. Thank goodness she was far away from him now.

"It was hot inside and I needed some fresh air, that's all," she said.

Charlene sighed and turned around in the passenger seat. "I can see why. D.J. Hatcher is one gorgeous man." She glanced at Mark. "Not as handsome as you, of course."

Her husband chuckled. "You'd better say that."

"You two looked like you were having a great time," Charlene continued. "It was a treat to see you happy. Did you give him your number?"

"No," Liza said. He hadn't asked. Her number was unlisted, and since Gram's last name was Haverford he'd never find her. Which was for the best.

Charlene looked disappointed. "I'm sorry."

Along with Gram and everyone else in the family, she thought three years alone was long enough for Liza. They all wanted her to date and fall in love with a good man.

And so did she, but she wished they'd leave her alone. "I don't like him that much, anyway."

"At least you're back in the game." Paul smiled. "I was beginning to wonder."

"That *is* good news," Mark said, grinning at her in the rearview mirror.

"You know how I feel about long-distance relationships. I'm not planning to date again until I get a job and know where I'm living."

Though Liza meant what she said, at the same time she wished D.J. *had* asked for her number. Flustered and confused, she chafed her arms.

Charlene smiled. "All the same, it's good practice."

Liza supposed she was right. "Listen, would you please not mention any of this to Mother or Gram?" There was no telling how either of them might react, and she especially wasn't up for negative comments from her mother.

Her cousins promised not to say a word.

"Speaking of your mother, you two seemed to get along okay at dinner." Mark again glanced in the mirror. "Does that mean you've finally made up?"

D.J. had asked her the same question, and Liza gave a similar answer now. "We'll never be close, but at the moment we're all right."

"Glad to hear it," Paul said.

The rest of the drive home, Liza and her cousins made small talk. But even though she participated in the conversation, her mind was elsewhere. Her intense and mixed-up feelings for D.J., a man she really didn't know that well, proved to her that she wasn't thinking clearly. The one thing she *was* sure about was that she wasn't likely to see him again until she flew back to Seattle. Given what had happened tonight, that was just fine with her.

AT EIGHT-THIRTY Saturday morning, looking disgustingly well rested, Carter Boyle sat across from him on the other side of D.J.'s battered office desk. He was there to help D.J. prep for his Monday morning meeting with Ryan Chase, the man who owned and ran Halo Island Bank.

"Late night?" Carter asked.

D.J. had worked with the accountant ever since he and Ethan had bought Island Air five years ago. When Ethan and Sheila had run off, Carter had helped D.J. deal with the mess they'd left behind. D.J. trusted the man, who was smart and closemouthed, and the only person other than him who knew about Island Air's dire financial situation. But they knew nothing about each other's personal life.

D.J. gave a wry smile and shrugged. "It was late, all right."

After Liza had walked away, he'd returned to the Gull's Nest to babysit Kiki—no fun at all—until the band finished for the evening.

Through the window behind Carter, he watched a turbine Otter taxi and lift off into another beautiful June sky. A flawless day for such a painful meeting. Knowing what was coming—a frank discussion about Island Air—and wanting to put off the bad news a little longer, D.J. stood up. "I need coffee. Want some?"

"Sure."

D.J. wandered into the small employees' kitchen. Mary, one of the airline's two dispatchers/reservationists, had made coffee when she came in earlier, bless her. He found two mugs and filled them, all the while thinking about the previous night.

Feeling like a stern big brother, he'd made sure Kiki drank only coffee or water, and by the time they left she was more or less sober. With a quick word to Joe, to say that he was dropping off Kiki at Brianna's, he'd seen her home, then headed to his own place for what ended up being a rotten night's sleep.

What with his business worries and those dangerous feelings for Liza messing with his brain and stirring up his body, who could sleep? It was a good thing he wouldn't see Liza again, because he didn't need the distraction.

When he returned to the office, Carter was sorting through the ledgers and bills with a face as sober as a funeral director's.

Small wonder. The quarterly insurance premium was just about due, and it was a staggering sum. But with planes and pilots to insure, the cost always had been major. Paying that and meeting the payroll just about drained the bank account. Thank God for a never-ending stream of summer tourists. D.J. knew he could scrape by and even whittle away at his personal debt, if not for that humongous loan payment.

Damn, but he wished he could figure out how to pay that. He set down his mug. "There isn't much hope, is there?"

"That's up to Ryan Chase and what he thinks of these." Carter gestured at the tax returns and quarterly financial statements.

D.J. doubted anything positive would come of it. Thanks to the personal debt his ex had saddled him with and a heap of late payments, his credit rating was a sorry mess, which likely ruled out another loan. If he owned his place, he'd have used it for collateral. But having sunk every penny into the business, he rented. Even the land Island Air sat on had been rolled into the bank loan.

Leaving him with an aging pickup, a decade-old Harley motorcycle and the cheap furniture in his studio apartment. Pathetic.

Still, he had to ask. "You think Chase will roll over my loan?"

"You already know the answer to that."

"Well, a guy can hope."

"Better to be realistic. Ryan'll suggest that you find yourself a partner with money."

After what happened with Ethan, D.J. had sworn off business partners. He set his jaw. "You know how I feel about that."

"Then you'd better be prepared for the other option. Selling."

For the past five years, Island Air had been D.J.'s sole reason for getting up in the morning. That he had to sell now hurt so bad, he couldn't stay still. "We about done here?"

"Yep. Let me know about that Monday-morning meeting." Carter left his half-empty mug on the desk.

After the accountant left, D.J. set the mugs in the dishwasher. *Loser,* his mind taunted. Hadn't the old man, now long dead, called him that often enough? Every time he got drunk, which was more often than not. Sheila hadn't believed he'd make it, either. His mom, also gone, had believed in him, though.

Damn, but he wanted to prove her right and his father and Sheila wrong, by making a huge success out of the business.

In a dismal mood he locked his office. Motorcycle helmet in hand he ducked into the front area, where Mary wielded the phones and the radio like a pro. She'd been with the company since it was a one-plane operation, before D.J. had bought it, and she knew the business almost better than he did.

She had no idea how bad off things were, though. And D.J. wasn't about to tell her just yet. "I'm taking off," he said.

She saw his face and frowned. "Bad meeting with Carter?"

The worst, but nothing D.J. hadn't expected. His heart feeling like a stone in his chest, he flashed a grin. "The usual. Call, if you need me."

"Will do. See you Monday."

"I'll be in late, around ten." After that meeting with Ryan Chase.

"Okay, boss." She gave him a trusting smile that hurt.

Halfway to the parking lot, D.J. changed his mind and headed for the hangar, a hundred yards away. He opened the gray door and walked inside. At the moment all five planes were out and the massive metal building was empty. The concrete floor was swept clean and the maintenance tools were neatly arranged at each of three worktables at three stations, ready for the fifty-hour, hundred-hour and annual maintenance and safety checks required for each plane.

Standing in the middle of the large space, he inhaled, taking in the faint scent of engine oil. Airplanes were his life, and damn, but he needed to fly today. Too bad all five planes were booked solid. Plus, he'd already put in his six days this week. No piloting for him until tomorrow.

The Harley was parked on the far side of the lot. D.J. pulled on his helmet and goggles. Swung his leg over the black leather seat then revved the motor. Enjoying the noise and the vibration and keeping an eye out for cops, he roared onto the street and sped toward home, using back roads to avoid traffic. Not counting flying, riding the bike was the best feeling in the world. The wind against his face was invigorating.

But it wasn't good enough to wipe away his troubles. D.J. thought about Joe and the rest of the pilots. Mary, and Sue, the other dispatcher. The mechanics and various other employees, all of them depending on Island Air to support them and their families.

What would happen to them if he sold?

What would happen to *him?* He'd have to move off the island he loved, to a big city where no one knew him and wouldn't know he'd failed.

With his mood so dark he couldn't go back to his small apartment, where the walls would close in on him. As a kid he'd turned to books to escape, when life at home got too ugly. He always carried a book with him, even now. At the moment, an Ernest K. Gann aviation novel was packed in the satchel strapped to the bike. He'd grab lunch from the deli, head for Halo Island Park, find a good tree to lean against and lose himself in the story.

And maybe get good and drunk tonight.

AS LIZA EXITED the building housing Sunset Manor's reception area and dining room, the sounds of kids playing and laughing at Halo Island Park filled the air. After being inside, the noon sun was bright and she had to shade her eyes.

Drawn by the expansive grounds, leafy trees and the children's play area, Annabel and Wilson raced toward the park, which was directly across the street. Mark and Charlene followed in hot pursuit, Mark carting an enormous jug of lemonade he'd taken from the van and Charlene bearing a sack filled with plates, napkins, cups and eating utensils. Behind them, Jake and Paul shared the weight of the cooler, which was filled with the picnic foods Liza and her grandmother had cooked and packed.

The whole family was here except for Diane and Art, who were meeting with their travel agent. But they'd promised to show up in time for the picnic lunch and Gram's announcement.

In no hurry, Liza hooked her arm through her grandmother's. Slowly, they made their way down Sunset Manor's gently sloping concrete walkway. Gram had always been a bustler, striding energetically wherever she went, and this snail-like pace was both shocking and worrisome.

Again Liza wondered if her grandmother was sick. And prayed that she wasn't. But if she was, wouldn't she be moving into one of the rooms designed for those who needed more care instead of her own apartment in a separate building?

"Now that you've seen Sunset Manor, what do you think of it?" her grandmother asked.

Liza thought about the one-bedroom apartment Gram would move into in exactly one month. At the moment it was torn apart for remodeling, but it had lots of windows and she could see that it was nicely laid out. Still, it was so small compared to Gram's two-story home. No yard to maintain, either, but there was a patio for flowers. Lucky for her grandmother, the patio and living room faced the park.

"It's light and cheerful, and suits your personality," she said. "I like it, Gram."

"I'm awfully glad. We have our work cut out for us with this move, don't we?"

"That's what I'm here for." Liza intended to do everything she could to make the move as painless and easy as possible. "I thought I'd get to work stripping wallpaper Monday morning, but if you'd rather I work on something else instead, just say so."

"That's fine. While you work on the upstairs, I'll start sorting through the downstairs closets." Her grandmother glanced at the rest of the family, a dozen yards ahead. "Thank you for keeping me company."

"It's my pleasure."

With such a beautiful day and most of the family together, a person couldn't help but be in a good mood. Liza had hardly even thought about D.J. Hatcher. At the moment he was the farthest thing from her mind, and the hunger and yearning of the previous night had all but faded away.

The instant Liza had opened her eyes this morning she'd put her mixed-up feelings behind her. Proving that the attraction between her and D.J. had been a one-time, in-the-moment event, just as she'd told her cousins.

To affirm to herself that she felt wonderful, no hard feelings over anything, today she'd dressed in bright clothes, a scooped-neck, cap-sleeved fuchsia blouse and capris from the closet. The sun felt good on the exposed skin of her collarbone and arms, ankles and calves.

She would give away the dull clothes, she decided, go shopping and get herself a few attractive outfits. For her next teaching job. Once a school district hired her.

As they entered the park Gram pointed ahead, past groups of teenagers, adults and active children. "Look, they found a table in the shade. This is our lucky day."

Mark, Uncle Jake and Paul moved off with the twins, heading for the playground just past a thick stand of trees. Charlene stayed behind to set up the table.

Liza was still thinking about the impending move. "You won't be able to fit much of your furniture into your apartment. What are you going to do with the rest of it?" she asked as they reached the picnic table.

Before her grandmother could answer, Charlene, in the process of spreading a checkered vinyl tablecloth over the wooden table, nodded at a distant shade tree. "Isn't that D.J. Hatcher?"

To Liza's surprise, it was. Wearing his aviator sunglasses, his back against the trunk, he was munching a sandwich and reading. Absorbed in the book, he looked as if he'd completely forgotten where he was.

She hadn't pictured him as a reader. She'd always considered men who enjoyed reading as much as she did to be sexy. But with or without a book, D.J. was sexy. His long legs, encased in jeans, were stretched out and crossed at the ankle. His T-shirt emphasized his broad shoulders and lean, hard torso. In short, he was pure masculine beauty.

All those intense, needy feelings came rushing back, stronger than ever. Her heart lifted as it had last night, and she let out a dreamy sigh. Caught herself and frowned. "What's *he* doing here?"

"I don't know." Charlene glanced at Liza, her eyebrows arching. "Hmm."

"You both seem to know this D.J. Hatcher," Liza's grandmother said, looking curious and intrigued. "Who exactly *is* he?"

Liza was reluctant to share because she didn't want any of this to get back to her mother. Who knew what she would say? Something mean, such as, "If Timothy didn't want you, why in the world would attractive, successful D.J. Hatcher?" Maybe not quite as callous as that, but with Diane you never knew.

"He was at the Gull's Nest last night," Liza said. "End of story."

"Ah." The older woman checked out D.J. "He likes to read, I see. That's a lovely habit. He's good-looking, too, even wearing those sunglasses. What you girls would call a hunk—am I right?"

Understatement of the year. The man was knockout gorgeous. But Liza said nothing.

"I certainly think so," Charlene said. "Not only is he handsome, he also owns Island Air. He was Liza's pilot yesterday."

"Really? I love Island Air. Flew it myself last time I visited Liza." She smiled. "I'd like to meet him."

As if D.J. heard the words, he looked straight at Liza. Or she thought he did. With those sunglasses, it was hard to tell. Her heart knew, though, and began to thud loudly.

"I'll introduce you," Charlene said. Waving, she beckoned D.J. over.

He closed the book and pushed to his feet. Slid the paperback into his hip pocket, grabbed his motorcycle helmet, tossed his lunch into a trash bin and started toward them.

More than one woman and several teenage girls watched his long-limbed stride with open interest. So did Liza. She definitely had a crush on him. A big crush. Which wasn't at all wise, but there it was.

Seconds later he stood before her. "Twice in two days." He shook his head, then tugged off his sunglasses. "Hello, Liza. Charlene."

"Hi." Charlene actually blushed. Even she was under his spell.

Who could resist those expressive gray eyes or the slight quirk of his sensual mouth?

Gram elbowed Liza and she made the introductions. "This is my grandmother, Mrs. Haverford. Meet D.J. Hatcher."

"Hello, D.J." Not the sort of woman who shook hands, Gram simply smiled. "It's a pleasure to meet the owner of Island Air."

"That's me."

Liza swore D.J. winced, which was odd. But the pained look was gone so fast that she guessed she must have imagined it.

"Happy to meet you, Mrs. Haverford. You're moving in to Sunset Manor, right?" He nodded at the glass-and-wood buildings. "Liza told me about that last night."

"She talked to you about me?" As Gram glanced from Liza to D.J., a calculating expression crossed her face.

D.J. nodded. "My grandmother lives in a retirement community in Dubuque, also near a park."

"Does she like it?" Gram asked.

"Loves it. I hope you will, too."

"Oh, I intend to."

He eyed the table, then shifted his weight. "Looks as if you're about to have a picnic. I don't want to intrude."

"Heavens," Gram said. "We won't be eating for a while yet, not until Liza's mother and stepfather arrive. We'd invite you to join us, but there are family matters to discuss. Some other time, I hope?"

While Liza choked with embarrassment, Charlene cleared her throat. "I was just about to join the rest of the family at the playground. Why don't you come with me, Gram."

"I'd love to. You two just go ahead and continue your visit." Gram smiled again. "It was nice meeting you, D.J., and I hope to see you again sometime."

"Uh, thanks." As they walked away, D.J. looked confused. "What was that about?"

"Isn't it obvious?" Liza rolled her eyes. "They think I should start dating again."

"You mean me?"

She sighed. "I'm afraid so."

Chapter Five

Of all the people to run into. After D.J.'s rotten morning, he was in no mood to meet Liza's grandmother or face Liza. He silently swore and nudged the grass with the toe of his sneaker.

"Am I that bad?" she said, and he realized he was scowling.

"Hell, no." He set his helmet on the picnic table bench, then looked her over, liking the pink top and calf-length pants that showed curves and some skin. Not enough of either, but enough to fire a man's imagination. And with sunlight filtering through the leafy tree overhead, dappling her hair and face, she was beyond pretty. "You look terrific."

"I do?" She seemed pleased and yet self-conscious. "It's not intentional. These clothes are old. They were in the closet and I wanted something colorful, so I…" Her cheeks flushed. "I'm babbling, aren't I?"

"Uh-huh." And it was cute. Hardly aware of his actions, he tucked her hair behind her ears, his fingers lingering there. "Relax."

She blew out a breath. "Okay." And locked her vast green eyes on his.

He lost himself in them. Her skin was as soft as he remembered. Suddenly, he wanted to kiss her, even more than he had last night.

He brushed his thumb across her soft lower lip. Her mouth opened a fraction and her eyes darkened, inviting him to do just that. His body jumped to life.

He was about to finally taste that mouth, when a Frisbee crashed to the ground inches from them.

They both jumped. D.J. turned away, scooped up the disk and tossed it to a scarlet-faced preteen boy who was loping awkwardly toward them.

"Sorry, mister," the kid said, neatly catching the thing.

"No problem. Just watch it next time."

D.J. was both relieved and disappointed. And poleaxed. It had happened again. He'd almost kissed Liza in front of a bunch of people, including her nearby relatives. Her grandma, for cripes sake. Was he nuts? He cleared his throat.

"Thing is, right now I have a lot going on." Such as, he was failing to save Island Air. No woman wanted to date a guy in his position. But even if the company had been in great shape, he wasn't about to get involved with Liza Miller. She'd been badly hurt before, and D.J. had no desire to hurt her again. Or to get hurt himself.

"If things were different and if I were looking to get involved, I would date you," he said, and he meant that.

"I'd date you, too—if we lived in the same town. But since we don't, and never will…" She shrugged.

This eased D.J.'s mind. He exhaled. "Then we're traveling on the same flight plan. That's good."

Liza glanced past him and cringed. "Uh-oh, here comes my family."

"My cue to cut and run." He grabbed his helmet. "Tell everyone I said goodbye."

Without a backward glance he strode toward the Harley.

As D.J. WALKED AWAY, Liza managed a wave and a calm smile for her approaching family. Inside, she was a mess. Not from their conversation, but because of the strong pull they both felt.

Amazingly, their mutual attraction seemed to have grown since the Gull's Nest. Only today there was no sensual beat of music, and no close body connection to blame for it.

Thrown by her powerful reaction to the man, upset over what it could mean and needing to *do* something, she reached for the plastic plates Charlene had placed at the end of the table. Liza was arranging them, trying to look composed, when Gram and the rest of the family reached her.

"Where did D.J. go?" Charlene asked, glancing around. "I wanted to introduce a real pilot to the twins and your uncle."

"He, um, had an appointment." Afraid someone would see how shaken she was, Liza focused on tucking napkins under the edge of each plate.

"Well, shoot." Charlene shrugged at Jake. "I guess you'll meet him next time."

Next time? Liza wasn't sure she could handle another encounter with D.J.

"Did you find out what he was reading?" Gram asked. "I'm always looking for a good book."

Liza shook her head.

"Well, what *did* you two talk about?" Charlene asked, her expression optimistic.

"Oh, this and that. We're not going to date, so please put that idea out of your heads." Refusing to talk more about D.J., Liza moved to the cooler. "Is anybody besides me hungry?"

"Me!"

"I am!"

Annabel and Wilson chimed at the same time.

"Can you wait just a little longer?" their great-grandmother asked. "Your aunt Diane and uncle Art will be here soon, and I'd like to hold off until then."

The truth was, Liza was too on edge to eat right now, anyway. She'd only wanted to change the subject. "That's fine," she said.

Charlene frowned at the twins' grimy hands and faces. "Why don't we stop at the bathroom and wash up? Maybe while we're gone, Aunt Diane and Uncle Art will show up. I'll take Annabel. Will you take Wilson, Mark?"

"Sure."

"I'll go with you," Paul said.

Uncle Jake shrugged. "My hands are dirty, too."

"Well, I wasn't digging in the sandbox with the rest of you," Gram said. "I'll stay here and help Liza set out the food.

"I like him," she said when the rest of the family was out of earshot.

No need to ask who she meant. Liza didn't care for the knowing smile on her grandmother's face. "Okay, but he lives here and I don't, and we're not going to date."

"And here I thought… Your expression when you first saw him under that tree."

Had her grandmother noticed that? Uncertain how to respond, Liza pretended to straighten a plate.

"Regardless, D.J. Hatcher is a good man."

"You only talked to him a few minutes. How can you tell?"

Gram reached for the plastic cups. "I've lived a lot of years. I can pretty much guess a man's character right away."

"You didn't guess about Timothy."

"Yes, I did. I never liked him."

This was news to Liza, and given Gram's habit of bluntly speaking her mind, it was also surprising. "Give me those cups and I'll fill them. Why didn't you say something?"

"Because you loved him, and so did your mother. I figured that in time I'd learn to do the same." Gram sighed. "Looking back, I wish I'd spoken up."

If she had, would things have turned out any differently? Along the way there had been plenty of danger signs that Liza herself had seen. Visiting Timothy on weekends and the frequent calls from his female classmates. Women flirting with him right in front of her, and the occasional smell of someone else's perfume on his clothing. Liza had been eager to get married, and Diane had been so pleased that her daughter was tying the knot with a plastic surgeon, that she'd ignored her misgivings. No, as determined as she'd been to get that ring on her finger, she would have dismissed Gram's warning.

"It probably wouldn't have made any difference." She filled a cup with lemonade, then handed it to her grandmother. "But from now on, if you see me about to make a huge mistake, will you please tell me?"

"I will. And if you have doubts, you know you can come to me."

They shared a warm look that made Liza feel much loved.

"I'd be so pleased to see you settled and happy," Gram said.

"I'm doing okay," Liza said, willing herself to believe that. "D.J. doesn't want a girlfriend, let alone a wife. He's been married before, and it was a bad experience for him."

"That doesn't mean he won't want to try again. The way he looked at you… Land, that takes me back to when your grandfather courted me." She placed her palm over her heart. "Either the man is already a little in love with you, or I'm out of my mind. And this old brain is as sound as the picnic table."

As they set out the containers of food, Liza half wished her grandmother was right. But already her feelings for D.J. were way too strong, and since she was leaving at the end of July…

"The man was your pilot yesterday," her grandmother continued. "Since then, you've seen him twice more. If that doesn't mean something, I don't know what does."

"What it means is, Halo Island is a small place. When I'm here, I always run into people I know." Two times was a fluke. Liza doubted she'd see him again, not with his busy job and the work on the house that she was about to settle into. "There is one more thing."

"What's that?" Gram sat down suddenly, looking exhausted.

That odd feeling that she might be sick, despite her denials, returned. Worry and sorrow welled in Liza's heart. Apparently her grandmother didn't want anyone to know, or she'd have said something. But someone needed to take action. Liza made a mental note to find out what was wrong and do something about it.

Gram was giving her an expectant look, waiting for her

to speak. "Would you mind not mentioning D.J. to Mother? Since there's nothing to tell."

Her grandmother pretended to lock her lips. "Mum's the word."

AN HOUR LATER, Liza and her family had enjoyed a leisurely lunch without a single mention of D.J. Hatcher. As the twins were attempting to climb the fat tree that shaded the table, Uncle Jake patted his round belly.

"Fried chicken, deviled eggs and cupcakes—another great meal. I'll have to go on a diet when I go home."

"What for?" Gram pursed her lips. "You're a fine, handsome man, and if the ladies can't see that…"

Jake flushed. "Spoken like a true mother."

"As your mother, I would love you to find the right woman and get married again."

She was full of romantic dreams for the family, and she wanted every single adult paired up—except for herself. Grandpop had been enough for her.

"I'm more concerned with my health," Jake replied.

There it was, the *H* word.

At once, Gram looked worried. "Are you sick, son?"

"No, but I had a physical a while ago. My doctor wants me to lose twenty pounds. Which is why these cupcakes are my last for a while."

"Twenty pounds." Gram made a dismissive gesture. "Is that all?"

"When was the last time *you* had a physical, Mom?" he asked.

Liza's grandmother narrowed her eyes at Diane. "What have you been telling him?"

Liza couldn't help but wonder if her mother and uncle knew something about Gram's health, after all. She glanced at Mark, Charlene and Paul, who shrugged and shook their heads.

Diane stiffened. "Since you never tell me a thing, there's absolutely nothing to say. You'd think that since I'm your daughter, you'd confide in me. But, no." She made a particularly dramatic face, for the sake of everyone at the table, Liza supposed. "That hurts me, Mother, it really does."

The sudden tension was difficult to ignore, but not all that uncommon. As usual, it was all about Diane.

Art murmured into her ear and patted her shoulder, and Diane nodded and gave an affected sigh.

Not about to leave the topic of her grandmother's health just yet, Liza steered the subject back. "You didn't answer Uncle Jake's question, Gram. Have you had a physical lately?"

Before her grandmother could answer, Wilson and Annabel rushed toward Charlene.

"Can we go back to the playground now?" Wilson asked.

"Why not." Looking delighted at the opportunity to get away from this tense discussion, Charlene started to stand.

Gram shook her head. "Please wait. There's something I need to say, and I want to do it while we're all together. It's time I made my announcement."

She seemed so drawn and somber, Liza's throat went dry.

To judge by the stricken looks on everyone but the twins, she wasn't the only one who was worried. No doubt sensing the solemnity of the moment, the twins sank meekly onto the grass without a peep.

"I did have a physical recently," Gram said. "And the

truth is, I do have a little heart condition. But it's nothing life-threatening."

Suddenly, the sun seemed to lose its brightness.

"Dear God." Diane covered her mouth with her hand.

Jake's normally ruddy color turned as pale as his mother's.

Liza sat still, slowly absorbing this information and wishing she could change it. Charlene, Mark and Paul looked equally at a loss.

If not for the other people in the park, a dark silence would have prevailed. Finally, Liza found her voice. "Oh, Gram," she said. "I'm so sorry. Are you on medication? Do you need surgery? Is there anything we can do?"

"Did you not hear what I just said? It isn't serious. I've started taking medication, yes, and I may need a bypass sometime in the next year or so. For now, Dr. Dove is watching me closely. There's also a cardiologist in Anacortes I'll be seeing from time to time. So I'm in good hands."

"Do you want Art and me to cancel our trip?" Diane asked.

"Heavens, no. I'll be fine. And if by some remote chance something goes wrong while you're gone, Liza will be here."

She shot a fond look Liza's way, making Liza especially glad she'd come.

"Is that why you're moving?" Paul asked.

Gram shook her head. "I was thinking about it long before this heart business showed up."

"Exactly when did it 'show up?'" Jake asked, giving his mother a dirty look. "Because this is the first any of us has heard of it."

"You mean, when did I find out about the heart problem? Exactly three days ago. Since everyone was coming here anyway, I thought, why not tell you all at the same time." She glanced at Diane. "You've been busy and excited planning your vacation. I didn't want to bother or worry you. So don't be hurt."

For once subdued, Liza's mother bit her lip and nodded. But Liza could see that she *was* hurt. And despite Gram's claim that she was all right, Diane was worried sick. They all were.

"In the year since I made up my mind to move, I've been doing a lot of thinking," Gram said in the heavy silence. "Diane and Art, I think your home is lovely."

At this non sequitur Liza's mother and stepfather looked confused. "Thank you," Diane replied.

"And yours, Jake, is too masculine for my taste, but it's comfortable enough." Gram glanced at Mark and Charlene. "When I visited you in Tucson a few years ago, I was impressed with your wonderful trilevel. And I've seen those pictures of your brand-new townhouse, Paul. Of course, I'd like to see you happily married someday, but for now almost everyone in the family is comfortably settled." Gram turned to Liza. "Except for you."

With all eyes on Liza, she felt as if she'd been put under a microscope and found lacking. As the only member of the family without a job or a permanent home, and the only one who'd been stood up at the altar, maybe she was.

Prickling at the thought, and aware of her mother's scrutiny, she straightened her back. "I'm doing just fine," she said loud enough that she almost convinced herself. "So don't worry about me."

"I'm not at all worried, dear. You're smart, strong and beautiful, and you always manage to land on your feet. But having once more lost your job, you'll have to find another place to live and put down roots all over again. That's not so easy."

The last thing Liza wanted was for her grandmother or anyone else in the family to be concerned about her. "It's not that bad, really. Once I land a job, I'll find a place to live and make new friends. Just as I have before."

"Roots are important," Gram said. "Don't you agree, Diane and Jake?"

"Sure," Jake agreed. "That's why I live in Portland." Where Liza's grandfather had come from.

"And why I stayed on Halo Island." Diane glanced at her husband. "And why Art moved back here after his wife died."

Gram nodded before again training her gaze on Liza. "Everyone in this family has put down roots someplace, except for you. You need a place to call home."

When Liza was younger and had believed in fairy tales, she'd always imagined owning her own home with a husband and filling it with kids. Timothy had almost killed that dream, but Liza remained hopeful. *If* she was lucky, maybe she'd have all that. In any case… "When I get a continuing contract, I'll probably buy myself a condo."

"Why wait?" her grandmother asked. "You've always loved my home as much as I have. Why don't you make life easy. Find a teaching job here and move into the house."

"What?" Realizing that her mouth was hanging open, Liza shut it. She knew everyone else was just as surprised.

"I was planning to leave it to you after I die, but now that I'm moving out and you're between jobs—well, the timing couldn't be better."

This explained why she'd encouraged Liza to choose the colors for the upstairs. Overcome with feeling, Liza blinked back tears. "That's way too generous, Gram. And while I thank you from the bottom of my heart, I also have to say that it's not fair. What about Mark and Charlene and Paul? And Mother and Uncle Jake?"

"Art and I don't want the house," Diane said, and Art nodded in agreement.

Uncle Jake shook his head. "Me neither."

"Charlene and I are happy where we are," Mark said.

"Same here." Paul turned to Liza. "Gram's right— you've always loved that house. It makes sense that you live in it."

Liza swallowed thickly. "I don't know what to say."

Her grandmother smiled. "Say, 'thank you, Gram.'"

"Thank you so much, Gram. But even if I wanted to live on the island, I can't. Not without a teaching job." And with her mother mere miles away. "There aren't any openings here. I've checked."

"You never know" was the reply. "If I were you, I'd go over to the administration office and talk to them."

But D.J. lives here. The thought of living in the same small town, where she could bump into him any time, was disconcerting, to say the least. "Can I think about it?"

"Certainly. If you decide you don't want the house, I'll just put it on the market in the fall. I'm in no hurry, so you have a few months to make up your mind. And I agree that giving you the property isn't fair to your cousins. To make things even, I have something for you, Mark and Paul.

"You don't know this, but years ago, your grandpop took out interest-bearing life insurance policies for each of you. The values have grown to substantial amounts. I'd like you to have the money from those policies now, so that I can watch you enjoy it. Liza, if you do take the house you'll sign over your policy to me. I don't need the money, but that keeps everything equal."

Gram made perfect sense. Liza nodded.

Stunned, her cousins sat silent a moment.

"Are you sure about this?" Mark asked, looking as if he might cry.

"Absolutely. I've already arranged everything with the insurance company. They're supposed to cut the checks and mail them at the end of the month." Looking pleased with herself, Gram folded her hands on the table. "Now for Diane and Jake. You're welcome to any of the furniture I don't need, and anything in the curio cabinet. There are some valuable pieces I think you should have. After you choose what you want, the rest of you should feel free to do the same."

It felt as if Gram was giving away her life. Even if it was to her loved ones, it was depressing. No one spoke.

Finally, she broke the silence. "Will somebody please say something?"

Jake straightened up. "When you drop a bomb, it sure is a dandy."

Chapter Six

Monday morning, Ryan Chase, a nice-looking guy about D.J.'s age, folded his hands on his huge, mahogany desk and looked genuinely regretful. "You're doing a decent job with Island Air. But with your credit score, there's no way we can roll over the loan."

The single shred of hope D.J. had harbored dissolved in a rush of shame, and he was sure he could hear his old man cackling, "Didn't I tell you?" Keeping his face blank, he nodded. "What are my options?"

"Take on a partner with enough money to pay the amount due. Or sell."

Carter had given him the same advice. D.J. liked and respected both men, but damned if he wanted to do what they said. Or sit here one more second. "I still have two months. I'll let you know." He pushed back his chair and stood. "Please don't tell anyone about this."

"Bank business is strictly confidential," Ryan assured him. Before opening the door to his office, he said, "If you decide to put the company on the market, don't wait too long. Businesses often take time to sell, and you don't want to go into foreclosure."

In a foul mood, D.J. steered the Harley toward Island Air. He wasn't sure what to do, but he knew he should tell his employees what was happening. Since they didn't have a clue. He dreaded admitting how badly he'd screwed up. But they were loyal, good people and they deserved the truth. Even if it meant they'd look at him as if he was a loser.

Grimacing at the thought, he braked at a stop sign. The best thing to do was get it over with quickly, he decided. He'd call an all-staff meeting for Wednesday morning.

TUESDAY NIGHT, after flying the maximum eight hours and spending a good hour on paperwork, then scarfing down two burgers, D.J. was dead tired. He really needed a good night's sleep. Yet he wasn't ready to head home. It was too quiet there. All that silence, and the walls seemed to close in on him.

Try as he might, he had yet to figure out a way to hold on to Island Air. Which turned his stomach. The burgers he'd had for dinner felt like lumps in his belly, and now he wished he hadn't eaten. Telling his employees tomorrow was going to be awful, and D.J. knew that the only way he'd sleep tonight was to stay out late and drink too much.

Lengthening his stride, he headed for Toddy's on Main Street. At nine o'clock in the evening the sun was edging closer to the horizon, but there was still plenty of daylight. This was the heart of the tourist area, and they were out in force, the bustle and noise helping to blunt his despair. But not entirely.

He'd scheduled the all-company meeting for bright and early the next morning, before the first flights of the day. D.J. had never held a companywide meeting during the busy season, and everyone knew something was up. So far he'd dodged his employees' questions. Even Joe's. That hadn't been easy, but D.J. wanted them all to hear the bad news at the same time.

On the way to Toddy's he passed Handy Mandy's Hardware Store. With barely a thought, he glanced through the big glass window.

Was that Liza Miller at the counter?

He stopped and then backed up, until he was facing the window like a kid mesmerized by a Christmas display. Yep, there she was. Wearing a baseball cap, with her hair in a ponytail, in jeans and a man-size work shirt, she was anything but attractive. Yet his heart tripped over itself.

D.J. frowned. This was the third time in five days that he'd run into her, and he was beginning to wonder. Bad enough to come across her at the Gull's Nest and the park. But tonight? At the moment he could barely stand his own company, let alone tolerate hers.

She was busy at the counter and didn't see him. He could walk on and she'd never know.

He meant to do that. But instead, fool that he was, he hovered by the door and waited. Less than a minute later, she shouldered her way out hefting two gallon-size cans of paint, a bulky bag of supplies and her purse. She was so loaded down, he wondered how she'd made it through the door.

The second she spotted him, her eyes widened and she stopped dead. Tourists gawked and went around them.

"D.J. What are *you* doing here?"

"Believe me, I didn't plan this. I was on my way to Toddy's Bar down the street."

Up close, he saw stains on her shirt and on her Bellingham Little League baseball cap. There was a dirt smudge on her cheek. He thought about wiping it away, but last time he'd touched her he'd almost lost it. He wasn't about to tempt himself again.

"You look like you could use a hand." He took the cans from her with barely a brush of the fingers, leaving her with her purse and the hardware store bag.

"Thanks. My car is around the corner."

Side by side they headed forward.

"What are you doing with all this stuff?" he asked.

"Getting ready to paint the upstairs of my grandmother's house. I spent yesterday and today stripping off fifty-year-old wallpaper you wouldn't believe. The glue was miserably stubborn." She glanced at her shirt and made a face. "That's why I'm such a mess."

"I think you look cute." The words just slipped out.

"Ha, ha. Very funny."

D.J. wasn't about to explain that he meant it. "Your grandma's getting ready to sell the place, huh?"

"I'm not sure yet." A crease formed between her brows, making her look both thoughtful and confused.

He told himself he wasn't interested in whatever was on her mind, but he asked the question all the same. "Not sure about what?"

"Selling. Gram offered her house to me."

"She did? You mean you might move to the island?"

That rattled him. If she lived here he'd keep running into her, and he wasn't sure he could handle that. Until he remembered. As soon as Island Air was sold, he'd be out of here.

"I haven't decided." Liza bit her lip. "If I don't take the

house, Gram will sell for sure. It's such a beautiful place, right on the beach, and I know she'd get a bundle for it."

"Does she need the money?"

Liza shook her head. "She wants to *give* it to me."

"Wow." D.J. was seriously impressed. "What do your cousins say about that? Or do they know?"

"She told us all Saturday at the park, not long after you left. Paul and Mark are getting big checks instead."

D.J.'s grandma didn't have that kind of money. He'd never cared at all, but at the moment he wished she was a millionaire, because he sure could use a big pile of cash. Instead, she was barely getting by, and hell, even if she were rich, he'd never take money from her. He wasn't made that way.

"That's one generous grandma you have."

"I know. The car's around the corner."

They turned onto Water Street and headed down the gently sloped sidewalk that ended at the beach, passing a dozen colorful booths selling tourist items on the way.

"I'm still in shock," Liza said. "I never imagined that Gram wanted me to have the house."

"Do you like it enough to move in?"

"I lived there my last two years of high school. There's nothing better than a house on the beach, especially a roomy cottage like Gram's."

"Then, what's stopping you? Besides your job in—" he glanced at her cap "—Bellingham."

Liza looked at him as if he'd asked how many letters were in the alphabet. "My mother lives on the island, remember?"

"I thought you said you and she were okay."

"We are getting along, but that doesn't mean things are

good between us. She's not easy to be around. And I *had* a job in Bellingham. Sadly, at the end of the school year I was laid off."

"Bummer. Maybe you can teach on the island."

"I checked yesterday, and again this morning. There aren't any openings."

"Maybe you can do something else," D.J. suggested.

"Not teach? That'd be like you not flying."

"Ah. Well." Toddy's Bar was back the way they'd come, and D.J. wanted badly to head there. "Where exactly is your car?" he asked.

"The next block down. I couldn't find a parking place any closer."

The paint cans were heavy, and that bag she was hauling didn't look light, either. "You were planning on carrying all this stuff all this way? By yourself?" He snorted. "Bet you're glad I came along."

"I could've managed it." Seconds later she glanced at him. "But thanks for happening to walk by. It's been a few days since I've seen you."

"I know. It's weird how we keep bumping into each other."

Talking to Liza felt great. D.J. was actually enjoying himself.

She nodded at a hulking gold Buick Riviera. "There's the car."

No wonder she'd parked so far away—finding a spot for a car that big during tourist season couldn't be easy. She set her bag on the sidewalk and unlocked the door, while D.J. checked out her wheels. The Buick appeared to be in mint condition—at least the paint job and hubcaps.

He whistled. "Some car."

"It's my grandmother's. She's had it since 1963. It only has 43,000 miles on it."

He set the paint cans on the floor in the back and checked out the almost pristine wheat-colored upholstery. "Sweet."

"She's always taken good care of her things."

Liza placed her bag of supplies beside the cans, then closed the door.

Leaving the two of them face-to-face, with nothing more to say. It was awkward, and D.J. shoved his hands into the pockets of his jeans. Liza tugged down her baseball cap, then wrapped both hands tightly around the strap of her shoulder bag.

"Um, thanks again, D.J.," she said.

He nodded. Time to head for Toddy's and a big cold one—or three.

"Want to go for a beer?" he asked. Then swore silently. He wanted to get away from Liza, not spend more time with her.

"I'd rather take a walk along the beach. It's only another two blocks." She gestured westward, as if he didn't know where the sound was. The salty sea smell alone was a dead giveaway. "The sun's about to set, and I'd hate to miss that."

"You would, huh?"

"Uh-huh." She locked her purse in the trunk and pocketed the key.

The next thing D.J. knew, he was walking beside her, headed for the beach.

LIZA HAD NO IDEA why she'd invited D.J. to enjoy the sunset. She could've watched it from Gram's, as she had every evening since she'd arrived, only there wasn't enough time to get there before dark. Or she could have walked to this beach and watched by herself.

But D.J. was fun company, and after two days spent alone wrestling with wallpaper, she needed some relaxation. She wished she'd put on makeup, changed her clothes and fixed her hair, but she hadn't planned on seeing him. By this point she ought to know better. Well, it was too late now.

Gram expected her back soon, and she didn't want her to worry. She glanced at D.J. "I should call my grandmother to tell her where I am, but I left my cell phone in my purse. May I borrow yours?"

"Sure." He slid his phone from his hip pocket.

Gram picked up on the third ring. "Hello," she said, sounding out of breath.

Had she raced to catch the phone or was this a symptom of her heart problem? Her heart, Liza guessed, and felt both helpless and uneasy. But Gram had assured her several times that everything was under control, and she had no choice but to believe that.

"Hi, honey, and what good timing," Gram said. "Tina Chase just phoned to invite you to dinner at her house Friday night. I hope you don't mind that I gave her your cell-phone number."

"I'm glad you did. Would you mind if I accepted her invitation?"

"Not at all. Why are you calling, when you'll be home soon?"

"That's just it. I won't be back for a while. I'm going to the beach off Water Street to watch the sunset."

"Good, because I'm sitting here in the living room,

looking out, and tonight's show will be spectacular. What a shame you don't have anyone to share the beauty with."

"I do." Liza glanced at D.J., whose head was cocked as he listened. Of course, he could only hear her end of the conversation. "I, um, ran into D.J. Hatcher outside the hardware store."

He shrugged and gave her a goofy who'd-have-figured smile that warmed her heart and made her like him even more.

"You did?" Gram sounded way too pleased. "Tell him hello."

"Gram says hello."

"Hi, Mrs. H."

"Now, *that* I heard," Gram said. "Mrs. H. How charming. Say, ask him about that book, will you?"

"Gram wants to know the name of the book you were reading the other day."

"*The Bad Angel,* by Ernest Gann. He was a pilot who lived on one of the islands and wrote adventure books about flying."

"Did you hear that, Gram?"

"I did. Tell him thank-you—I just might pick up a copy. Well, I won't keep you any longer, and I won't wait up. You two have fun."

Liza could almost see her grandmother's knowing wink. Suddenly, she felt like a teenager out on a date, reporting to her mother. But she was no innocent adolescent, Gram wasn't her mother and this wasn't a date. It was simply a matter of enjoying the sunset with someone she'd bumped into. As she hung up and returned D.J.'s phone, she rolled her eyes.

"Uh-oh," he said. "Don't tell me she thinks there's something going on between us."

There was no reason to hide the truth. "I'm afraid so, but as long as we both know there isn't, we'll be fine."

If you ignored the strong undercurrent of sexual attraction. Even now, making casual conversation, Liza's body felt tense and alive.

"Right," D.J. said. "We're friends, period."

"About to enjoy the sunset together. We'd better hurry, *friend,* or we'll miss the whole thing. Come on."

They jogged the rest of the way to the beach, where, slightly winded, they joined a throng of adults and children facing the horizon. The sun was almost down, turning the pale blue sky brilliant with streaks of vivid pink and gold. At this angle Liza could actually see it dropping. Whitecaps danced over the darkening water, birds called out and circled overhead and waves shushed gently as the tide slowly went out.

So romantic, she thought, shooting a quick glance at D.J. He was close enough to reach out and… *He's a friend and only a friend,* she sternly reminded herself. And took a small sidestep away, so that she was in no danger of sinking against him.

The warm air was ebbing faster than the daylight. Wearing only a cotton shirt, Liza wrapped her arms around her middle.

"Cold? I'll warm you up." D.J. closed the safety gap she'd created and slipped his arm around her shoulders. "Just don't tell your grandma about this."

"There's nothing to tell, right?" Liza said.

She sounded perfectly normal, but her insides were a

tangle of fear, longing and need. Her heart bumped hard, heat pulsed through her and she knew that, friends or not, before the night was over she would kiss D.J. Hatcher.

WATCHING THE SUNSET with Liza was fantastic. Maybe because her hair smelled so good. Or because she fit so well against his side. At the moment, D.J. was so into her that he barely noticed the sky. He forgot about his money problems, forgot that he was on the verge of deciding to sell his life's blood. At the moment, all he cared about was Liza.

Did she share any of his fever? He glanced at her, but thanks to the bill of her baseball cap, he couldn't see her face. He slid his hand down her arm, past the sleeve of her shirt, to her skin. Stroked his palm down and up, pushing the sleeve toward her shoulder. And swore she was shivering. No goose bumps, but he felt her quiver.

"Still cold?" he asked close to her ear, his voice gruff with his growing need.

Now she looked up at him, her eyes big and warm, telling him that yes, she also felt the current between them. "No. I'm not."

He couldn't look away, and neither could she. She turned to face him, suddenly so close that he could see the dark flecks in her irises and feel the warmth of her breath on his face. She smelled like peppermints. That turned him on, as well.

He smiled. "You thinking what I'm thinking?"

"I'm not thinking at all." She cupped his jaw with her slender fingers. "I just want you to kiss me, so I can stop fantasizing about it."

"You've been doing that, too?"

Behind them was a huge pile of driftwood. Without taking his eyes from Liza, still holding her close, he back-stepped her away from the crowd, into the deep shadows. Alone with her, sheltered by the jutting pile of wood, he at last did what he'd wanted to do for days.

Pulled off her cap and kissed her.

Her lips were soft and yielding. She tasted warm and eager, sweeter than he'd imagined. Her round breasts pressed against his chest, her hips inched closer to his groin and a certain part of him thickened and rose. Widening his stance and angling his head, he urged her mouth open and deepened the kiss.

Their tongues tangled. A small sound emerged from Liza's throat. Threading her fingers through his hair, she pushed against him, against his now-throbbing need. Blood roared in his veins. Fevered with the taste of her, he came back for more, and again, the kisses running together in one long, passionate mating of their mouths.

His hungry hands curled around her sweet behind, lifting and bringing the vee that sheltered the most sensitive part of her hard against his groin. She wriggled closer still, nearly killing him with the teasing slide of her hips. Hunger raged inside him, so that all he could think about was stripping naked, wrapping her thighs around his hips and…

What the hell are we doing?

Afraid of the intensity of his feelings and rattled by his lack of control, D.J. ended the kiss, let go of her and stepped back.

They were both breathing hard. He retrieved her cap

from the ground, slapped it against his thigh to get the sand out and placed it back on her head.

"Good thing we finally got that out of our systems," he said.

Liar. Now that he'd tasted her he wanted more. Lots more.

Liza touched her lips. In the last fleeting rays of light she appeared dazed—and as turned on as he was.

"I should get home," she said.

"I'll walk you to your car." Then, he'd head for Toddy's and that beer. An icy one to cool him down.

They left the beach and strolled the sidewalk in silence, not speaking again until Liza had unlocked the car.

"Good night, D.J.," she said, standing behind the open door as if it were a protective shield.

He understood. He wanted to touch her, but instead clasped his hands behind his back. "See you, Liza."

When the engine purred to life, he turned away and headed for Toddy's. On the way there he cursed himself for hanging around outside the hardware store. If he'd just passed by, tonight wouldn't have happened. For sure, it *shouldn't* have happened. Kissing Liza was a big mistake.

Because now that they'd started something, D.J. wasn't at all sure they could stop.

Chapter Seven

D.J. was in the conference room at six-thirty Wednesday morning, gearing up to tell his employees the truth about Island Air, when Joe wandered in.

"Morning," he said, looking rested and ready for a day of flying.

"Hey there." D.J. tried his damnedest to put on a happy face.

And earned a squinty-eyed look in return. "You look like hell, D.J." Joe shook his head. "What'd you do, tie one on last night?"

That had been the plan, only D.J. had been too shaken up by those kisses to sit at the bar. "It was only one beer."

Followed by a cargo load of tossing and turning. It wasn't every day that a man admitted he was a failure in front of his entire company. D.J. owed Liza for taking his mind off his troubles for a short while. Except that…

"Then some hot babe must've kept you up."

Emphasis on *up*. Joe had no idea how right he was, but D.J. wasn't about to share the story of his sexual frustration. Serious kisses and a whole lot of lust—exactly what he needed on his screwed-up, miserable, already full plate.

As far as he was concerned, what had happened between him and Liza was over and done with. He was not going near her again. It was too dangerous. That and the fact that once she heard about Island Air, any interest she might have in him was likely to fizzle and die. And on the island, word traveled fast.

No woman wanted to hang out with a failure.

Joe took one look at his face and raised his eyebrows. "This is gonna be a bad-news meeting, isn't it?"

Not about to answer that question just yet, D.J. nodded at the extra-large white box he'd brought from Mocha Java, a popular downtown café and bakery. "Have a doughnut, Joe. They're still warm."

That did the trick. Joe licked his lips and opened the box.

Other pilots, mechanics and the two dispatchers wandered in, shooting D.J. curious looks before they, too, dug in to the doughnut box and then found themselves seats.

Since the pilots needed to get to their planes by seven-thirty for their eight o'clock flights, D.J. began at 7:00 sharp. "I know you're all wondering why I called this meeting."

Standing at the front of the room, taking in their concerned faces, his heart seemed to sink into his gut. It would be easier to face a firing squad. But these were good people and they deserved to know the truth.

He cleared his throat. "It kills me to say this, but Island Air is in financial trouble. I may be forced to sell the business."

After a moment of stunned silence, Joe spoke. "That blows." He looked as if he'd been sucker punched. "You never said anything about this before."

Other employees voiced their agreement. Their shock and dismay were exactly what D.J. had expected. He'd thought he was prepared for their accusing looks. Not so, however, since at the moment he felt lower than pond scum.

"I wanted to tell everyone at the same time," he said. "That's only fair."

After a long, tense moment of silence, a fifty-something pilot named Mick Edwards crossed his arms over his chest.

"Just answer one question for me. We're doing so well, and have been for the past few years. How did this happen?"

D.J. wasn't about to explain that Ethan and Sheila had saddled him with more debt than he could handle. Most everyone here already knew all that stuff, and why rehash the past yet again?

He gave Mick and the others the bottom line. "There's a big loan payment due the fifteenth of August. I don't have the money, and short of robbing a bank I don't see any way to get my hands on it."

After a few moments of muttering and resentful looks that D.J. knew he deserved, he wanted nothing more than to turn around and walk out. Instead, he stayed put. "It's almost time to go to work, but we still have a few minutes," he said. "Are there any other questions?"

"I have one," Pat Drogger, one of the most seasoned mechanics, said. "We're busier than ever, and I know we're making money. What are you doing with it?"

In other words, "Are you stealing from the company or are you mismanaging it?" The implication stung like hell. D.J. wished he'd invited Carter to sit in on this meeting and explain for him.

"It costs a lot to run an airline," he said. "Insurance, labor, maintenance on the planes and buildings, property taxes, and growth—all of those things take money. We got off to a rocky start, and after paying the bills there's never been enough to set aside for this loan." Drogger looked unconvinced, but D.J. continued. "Look, if you don't trust me, take a look at the books. Hard copies of everything are in the file cabinet in my office. Or if you'd rather talk to my accountant, Carter Boyle, feel free to call him." D.J. made a mental note to alert Carter to expect phone calls.

Pat Drogger said nothing, but sat back, uncrossed his arms and looked satisfied.

"What about our jobs?" another pilot asked.

"Without everyone in this room, Island Air wouldn't even have lasted as long as it has or done so well. If I have to sell—and it's looking that way—I'll be letting whoever buys the place know how great you all are."

D.J. kicked the toe of his sneaker at a worn place in the blue carpet. Damn, he wished he could fly this morning. But he'd called in a sub so that he could work on the business side of the company and see if there wasn't something he could do that didn't involve taking on a partner or selling. Some idea Carter and Ryan Chase hadn't thought of.

"Can we talk about the financial problems outside this room or is it a secret?" Mary asked. Her broad, middle-aged face was full of concern.

"It's no secret," D.J. said. Not anymore.

Then the phones started ringing. Island Air was open for business, and the meeting was over.

"I'll keep you posted," he said. "If anybody wants to talk or look at the books, I'm here."

As the others filed out, Joe hung back. "You could've said something at the Gull's Nest the other night."

"Like I said, that wouldn't have been fair to everyone else. Besides, you and Brianna were so happy. I didn't want to ruin your evening." D.J. studied the face of his tense, angry friend. "Listen, if you want to punch me out, go ahead."

"Nah." Hands in his jeans pockets, Joe shrugged. "But damn, Deej, this bites."

Joe never had been the kind to carry grudges long. Which was a relief. The tightness in D.J.'s chest eased a fraction. "You said it."

"You gonna stay on?"

D.J. shook his head. "If I do have to sell, I'll leave town. Maybe move to a big city and become a flight instructor or something."

"Aw, man, you don't have to do that."

Yeah, he did. Staying and watching someone else run Island Air, knowing that his coworkers thought he'd failed, would hurt too much.

Starting over again. It was going to hurt, big-time.

MUSCLES LIZA DIDN'T even know she had twinged painfully as her flip-flops thwacked across the kitchen linoleum Wednesday morning.

Dressed and reading the *Halo Island Weekly,* Gram was sitting in her usual place on the banquette. Through the windows the blue sky and bright sun promised another perfect summer day.

And tonight, another spectacular sunset. Not as amazing as last night's, though, Liza thought. Kissing D.J. against the backdrop of the ocean and setting sun had been just about perfect. Even if it was foolhardy.

"Good morning, sleepyhead." Gram put down the paper and gave her a big grin.

"Morning," Liza returned, bracing herself for a host of prying questions.

Instead, to her relief, there were none. Yet.

"You missed a perfect halo cloud this morning." Halo Island was named for the halo-shaped fogs that sometimes formed above the water. "The coffee's made. Help yourself."

"Thanks." As Liza moved gingerly toward the coffee-maker, her grandmother's eyes narrowed. "You're in pain."

"It's nothing, really. I was fine when I went to bed last night." If you didn't count the physical longing that D.J. had awakened in her. Liza massaged her biceps. "I guess my muscles tightened up while I slept. From peeling wallpaper."

"Ah. Well, a hot shower will help."

Liza hoped so, because today she meant to plaster the cracks in the upstairs walls, sand them and apply primer. A job that was strenuous enough on a person's arms and back without preexisting aches and pains. As soon as she filled her mug with coffee and added some milk, she took a seat at the table.

She'd barely savored her first sip before her grandmother tilted her a curious look and started with the questions.

"Did you and D.J. have a good time last night?" she asked, her eyebrows arching as she said *good time.*

Had they ever. The man kissed like a dream. "It was okay," Liza said, blowing on her coffee to cool it.

"Only okay?" The older woman looked disappointed. "When will you see him again?"

"I don't know."

Which was the truth. Despite all those amazing kisses,

D.J. hadn't asked Liza for her number. She hadn't asked for his, either, mainly because every time she was with him she liked him more. If she wasn't careful, she could fall for him. Which would lead to nothing but heartache. And because growing feelings for him aside, if she saw him again, she had no doubt they'd share more of those delicious kisses—and who knew what else. With D.J., she couldn't seem to say no. Didn't want to.

At the sight of Gram's long face, Liza tried to explain, "D.J. and I are friends, Gram. You know he doesn't want a girlfriend, and I can't get involved in a long-term relationship just now." How many times did she have to explain? Apparently, at least a few more, until the words sunk in. "Besides, I didn't come to the island for romance, I came to help you." After holding her grandmother's gaze for a long, level moment, Liza neatly changed the subject. "So, what's on your agenda for today?"

"More sorting through things. While you were at the beach with D.J. last night, your mother called and offered to come over and help with the attic this morning. Wasn't that thoughtful?" Her grandmother must've seen the alarm on Liza's face, because she hastily added, "Don't worry, I didn't say a word about D.J."

"Phew." Liza hadn't seen her mother since Uncle Jake and her cousins had left the island Sunday afternoon. She didn't want to see her again so soon. This was what life would be like if she moved into the house—seeing way too much of Diane. "I thought cleaning out the attic was my job," she said. "Isn't that why I'm here?"

"Yes, but I'm not about to turn down your mother's help. Neither should you. Have you looked in there, lately?

The whole place is crammed with stuff—furniture and boxes I should've tossed long ago. If you'll bring down some of the boxes, I'll look through them. But I can't do much more than that. You need your mother's help, and working in the attic should give those sore wallpapering muscles a chance to rest."

Aching muscles seemed a small price to pay to avoid spending time with Diane, but since Gram had already arranged things… Liza sighed. "All right. What time will she be here?"

Gram checked her watch. "In about half an hour."

"So early?"

"Early? It's almost nine o'clock, missy. If I'd had my way, we'd have started hours ago."

"I could have set my alarm if you'd said something," Liza said.

"I didn't know until after you'd called last night. Besides, you needed your beauty sleep." Gram's mouth twitched. "Though I have to say that even though you slept in, you look tired."

"Do I?"

Small wonder. Liza hadn't exactly slept well. Who could settle down after those sizzling kisses? Once she finally had relaxed enough to fall asleep, the dreams had started—involving erotic scenes of her and D.J. doing all sorts of steamy, sexy things to each other. Even now, with her grandmother studying her, Liza's body felt fevered and needy.

Too antsy to sit, she stood and picked up her mug. "I'd better shower and dress before Mother shows up. I'll finish my coffee upstairs."

"What about breakfast? You have to eat."

"I'll grab something later. Unless you're hungry. I'm happy to cook you something."

"Heavens, no. I ate hours ago. You could invite him to dinner sometime."

Him meaning D.J. Liza frowned. Wait till he heard about this. But since they had no plans to get together, he wouldn't. Unless they bumped into each other. Which, given the number of times they'd done just that already, seemed a distinct possibility. "Didn't you hear what I said? We're friends and only friends."

Except friends didn't share passionate kisses or fantasize about each other with such fierce physical longing that they could hardly function. At least Liza couldn't.

"So what?" Gram waved her hand in the air. "Friends eat meals together all the time."

"Not D.J. and me." Liza could picture it now, D.J. at the dinner table and Gram shooting Liza and him knowing looks while she blatantly pushed them together. If Diane ever found out… Speaking of her mother, she'd be here soon. "I'm going upstairs now."

She went to get dressed, her thoughts on D.J. If she was smart, she'd protect her heart. Never mind that around him, she forgot what was safest for her. Next time they ran into each other, she'd keep her wits about her, say hello and then quickly walk the other way.

That ought to take care of the situation.

THE LATE-MORNING SUN was bright, and as D.J. exited the Island Air offices, he pulled his sunglasses from his shirt pocket. With his eyes hidden, he felt better. He'd spent the past two hours banging his head against the wall while he was supposed to be catching up on the paperwork that cluttered his desk. No one had stopped by with questions or to have a look at the books. D.J. figured the bad news hadn't sunk in yet. Or maybe they were too upset to face him right now.

D.J. sure was on edge. Damned if he could figure out a way to save his sorry butt. Carter and Ryan were right. It was either take on a partner or sell.

Both unacceptable options. Miserable, D.J. leaned against a wall on the shady side of the hangar. He watched tourists mill around on the sidewalk opposite the parking lot and wondered what to do with the next four hours. It was still morning, and he wasn't scheduled to fly until late this afternoon. Call him a coward, but he couldn't hang around here for one more second.

He needed a distraction, something to take his mind off his troubles. Alcohol was out, since he was flying today. He thought about reading more of *The Bad Angel,* but feeling as rotten as he did, there was no way he could lose himself in a book.

There was only one person who could give him what he needed. Liza Miller. She was sweet, fun and sexy, and D.J. badly wanted all that. Never mind that seeing her again wasn't the smartest idea.

He wasn't about to examine why she was the one he needed, either. He just did. News of a business in trouble didn't travel as fast as more personal stuff, and he figured it'd take at least a day or two to get to her. That bought him a brief chunk of time in which to go on pretending that all was well. At least he wouldn't see pity or disgust in her eyes.

Wasn't she painting at her grandma's? He'd call and ask her to lunch, someplace far away from Island Air. Two friends getting together.

Problem was, he didn't have her number. He glanced at the ground and swore. Then he remembered. She'd called her grandmother from his cell. He slid it from his hip pocket, retrieved the number and pressed the redial button.

DUST SWIRLED about her as Liza dragged a large cardboard box labeled Boys' Clothes across the attic floor. The lone window in the space wouldn't open, and the air was hot and stale. Liza wiped her brow with her forearm. She and her mother had been in the attic about an hour, but Diane's constant criticism had made it seem as if they'd been up here much longer. For her grandmother's sake, Liza let the comments go, but with each remark it became harder to do so.

As Liza sat on her knees to open the box, she tightened her ponytail and blew the stray wisps of hair out of her eyes.

Sitting cross-legged in front of stacks of dusty children's books, her mother, whose face was flushed with heat, noticed and pursed her lips.

"Long hair is so hot in the summer. Why don't you cut it while you're here? Maybe some highlights, too, to brighten up that dishwater color. I'm sure if I ask my stylist, Ruthie, she could squeeze you in."

"I like my hair long, thanks. And I don't want to color it."

"Suit yourself, but with your facial shape, short hair would be much more flattering."

Enough was enough. Liza bristled. "Do you realize that every word out of your mouth today has been critical of me? My clothes, my makeup, my career—and now my hair. Please stop it."

Diane's eyes widened in surprise. "Goodness, you're touchy."

But at least she held her tongue.

A quick rifle through the box of boys' clothes revealed well-used shirts and pants. Obviously, these things had been Uncle Jake's. They were so dated and worn, Liza doubted the thrift store would want them. Pulling a permanent marker from her pocket, she labeled the contents Trash. Then pushed the box toward their growing throwaway pile.

"There's some great furniture up here," her mother said, finally breaking the silence.

She was right. Grouped under the rafters, to one side, were an old maple rocking chair, a small brocade love seat and footstool, a pair of ornately carved end tables and a beautiful cane-back chair.

"Are you taking anything?" Liza asked.

"Only these children's books."

Who knew for what purpose. If Diane wanted grandchildren, it'd be a while.

"Your cousins and Uncle Jake don't want any of this stuff, either." Diane looked thoughtful. "You know, when we were growing up, all of these pieces were in the living room. After your grandmother takes what she wants to her apartment, you could have everything here refinished and use it downstairs. I'm sure she would love for you to use it. Then you can get rid of those cheap pieces you have in your apartment."

The dig about her thrift-store furniture aside, Liza's mother talked as if Liza would be moving into the house. A decision she hadn't yet made.

It *would* be wonderful to live near Gram and spend more time with her. But more time with Diane was another story. Then, there was the matter of finding a job. And her dangerous feelings for D.J. She didn't—

"Liza? Do you want this furniture or not?"

"I would, only I haven't made up my mind yet about moving here."

"Oh."

Though Diane's attention stayed on the books in front of her, she looked disappointed. Which was unexpected, given the fact she thought everything Liza did was wrong.

"How's the job search going?" she asked.

"Fine." Geesh, she was tired of that word.

Especially since it wasn't exactly the truth. She hadn't checked the job postings today, but a look yesterday had shown nothing except openings for a high-school counselor in Olympia, Washington, and two algebra teachers in Seattle. None of which Liza was qualified for.

Her mother was watching her closely, so she tried a reassuring smile. Diane frowned.

"Maybe you need further education. Lots of universities offer online courses. Summer term has just started, and I'm sure they'd let you in. This is the perfect time to start working toward becoming a principal."

Liza gaped at her. "I already told you I don't want to do that. I'm a teacher. Teaching makes me happy."

"I know you believe that." Her mother compressed her lips like a petulant child. "But I think if you—"

"You haven't said much about Australia. What cities do you and Art plan to visit?"

"All right, I'll stop nagging you. We're starting with the

big cities on the east coast—Sydney, Canberra and Melbourne, and then we fly west, to Perth. If you want, I'll show you the travel brochures."

"That'd be great," Liza said.

"We'll do it over dinner—you, me and Art. How about sometime next week?"

Liza didn't want to spend a whole evening alone with Diane and Art, but she couldn't very well say that. "All right, but remember what we discussed? I'd like to include Gram, and eat here. She probably wants to see the brochures, too."

"She's already seen them, but of course if—"

"Telephone, Liza," her grandmother called.

Relieved at the chance to get away from her mother, Liza jumped up. "Be right there."

In the kitchen, Gram was smiling. "It's D.J.," she said in a loud whisper.

Heart thudding, Liza took the phone. "Hello?"

"Uh, hi. How's the painting going?"

Liza turned away from her grandmother's curious eyes. "I'm working on the attic, instead. With my *mother.* Aren't you supposed to be flying?"

"Not for a few more hours. Thought you could use a break."

"You thought right."

"Have you eaten yet?"

"No."

"Have lunch with me."

Seconds later, confused, she hung up.

"Well?" Gram asked.

"D.J.'s on his way over to take me to lunch."

A grin lit her grandmother's face.

"It's not a date. Just two friends getting together." That's what Liza had told D.J., and he had readily agreed. She wouldn't think about her steadily growing feelings for him, or the fact that she really should steer clear of him.

"Of course," Gram said. "What are you standing here for? Go upstairs and get cleaned up."

Liza hesitated. "What about Mother?"

"What about me?" Diane said. She'd come downstairs without making a sound.

Gram didn't say a word, just raised her eyebrows and let Liza explain.

"I have lunch plans with a friend, and I need to get cleaned up," she said. "When he gets here, please be nice. In fact, don't say anything at all."

Chapter Eight

"Nice to meet you." Standing in Mrs. Haverford's cozy living room, D.J. extended his hand to Liza's mother. Now he knew where Liza had gotten that mouth. Except that her mother's lips were pinched.

"Hello," she said, letting him shake her hand. Her gaze slid coolly over his jeans, Island Air T-shirt and sneakers, as if she found fault with his clothes.

"See that T-shirt?" Liza's grandmother said. "D.J. owns Island Air."

She *would* have to mention that.

"Oh? How lovely." At last she smiled. "It's a pleasure to meet you, D.J. Running an seaplane company must be *so* interesting."

"It is." And right now, also painful as hell. Determined to forget about all that for the next little while, D.J. nodded at Liza. "We should go."

"Must you?" Liza's mother said, looking genuinely disappointed. "We've hardly had a chance to talk."

"D.J. has to go to work later." Liza moved toward the door, as if she couldn't wait to leave.

"Then we'll just have to get together some other time."
Shaking her head, Liza opened the door.

"Bye," her grandmother said.

Her mother smiled again. "Have fun, you two."

Liza made a face. "This isn't a date, Mother. Is it, D.J.?"

"Nah," he said. "Just two friends getting together for a few hours."

As they crossed the stone walkway toward the driveway, Liza groaned. "That was so uncomfortable."

"It wasn't that bad. Your mom liked me."

"Once she found out you owned Island Air. She was nice to you because you're a successful businessman. If you weren't, believe me, her behavior would've been a lot less friendly."

Would Liza's, too? D.J. figured he'd find out soon enough. He knew he should tell her about his situation. And he would. Just not this afternoon. Right now, he needed her to help him forget his problems for a little while.

They reached the Harley, which D.J. had parked beside a shiny Mercedes that probably belonged to Liza's mom.

"Um, I've never ridden a motorcycle," Liza said. "We could take Gram's car."

In no mood for the confinement of a car, even a vintage model, D.J. reached for the two helmets he'd brought along. "Trust me, you'll love the bike." He handed one to Liza. "Put this on. And your sunglasses."

"Do you like clams?" he asked when they were both ready to go.

"Love them."

"Good." He swung his leg over the seat. "Climb on, and hang on tight."

Her arms went snug around his waist. He turned the key, kicked up the stand and pumped the gas. The engine roared to life. Keenly aware of Liza molded to his back, D.J. sped off, adrenaline pumping. Despite the traffic, he managed to make good time. With Liza behind him and the wind whipping past, he felt great. This was exactly what he needed.

Ten minutes later he pulled up at Clams, a drive-up shack that was open only for lunch and served the freshest clams around. The line for service snaked halfway around the block.

D.J. idled the engine, pulled off his helmet, pushed up his shades and turned his head. "How'd you like the ride?"

"You were right." Liza, too, shed her helmet. "I'm loving it!"

The wind had brought color into her cheeks, and her eyes sparkled as bright as the ocean beyond them. She was so beautiful. He wanted to kiss her until the world faded away. But this was neither the time nor the place. That would have to wait until after lunch. Smart or not so smart, D.J. needed badly to taste her again.

"What'd I tell you?" he said, rolling the bike slowly toward the order window.

"I can't believe I've never done this before. It's wonderful. Thanks for the experience, D.J."

He'd never seen her so enthusiastic. Wished that joy was contagious, because he sure could have used some of it.

"Just wait," he said, figuring she'd like their picnic spot as much as he did.

Five minutes later he packed a fat lunch bag into the leather pouch attached to the side of the bike. "All set?"

Get FREE BOOKS and
FREE GIFTS when you play the...

LAS VEGAS
GAME

*Just scratch off
the gold box with a coin.
Then check below to see
the gifts you get!*

YES! I have scratched off the gold box. Please send me my **2 FREE BOOKS** and **2 FREE GIFTS** for which I qualify. I understand that I am under no obligation to purchase any books as explained on the back of this card.

54 HDL ENXH   **154 HDL ENXT**

FIRST NAME	LAST NAME

ADDRESS

APT.#	CITY

STATE/PROV.	ZIP/POSTAL CODE

(H-AR-03/08)

7	7	7	Worth TWO FREE BOOKS plus TWO FREE GIFTS!
🍒	🍒	🍒	Worth TWO FREE BOOKS!
🔔	🔔	☘	TRY AGAIN!

www.eHarlequin.com

Offer limited to one per household and not valid to current subscribers of Harlequin American Romance®. All orders subject to approval.

"Let's ride," Liza said, then gave a joyous laugh that had D.J. grinning.

Her arms wrapped around his middle once more and he took the hilly back roads to a rocky cove at the far end of the island. Huge stones littered the beach and jutted over the water, which made this an unpopular tourist spot. Just as he'd hoped, there was nobody around.

He pulled an old plaid blanket out of the storage pouch and handed it to Liza. Carrying their lunch and two bottles of pop, he led her forward. They squeezed through a gap between two mammoth boulders, then made their way to a giant rock that sloped gently over the water. Once they reached the top there was nothing in the way of an astonishing view.

"This is it." D.J. took the blanket from Liza and laid it over the smoothest part of the surface, which was warm from the sun.

Shading her eyes, Liza stared at the sea. "Wow," she murmured. "This is such a cool place."

"Thought you'd like it. I discovered it after my marriage fell apart. It's great when you want to be alone."

"I wish I'd known about this when I was a teenager. I'd have come here all the time. It's perfect, D.J. Absolutely perfect. I so needed this."

"Me, too."

Her words and the appreciation in her eyes made him feel fantastic. Enjoying the view, they said little while they ate their meal. D.J. kept his problems at bay by thinking about what might happen after lunch. He'd start things rolling with a kiss or two and see where that took them.

Finished at last, they tossed the remaining scraps to the herons, pelicans and wheeling gulls.

Now to get down to the important stuff. He slipped his arm around Liza's shoulders. She settled herself willingly against his side, giving him the warmth he so badly needed.

A soft sigh slipped from her lips.

"Hey there, Liza." He caught her chin in his hand and lifted her face.

"Hey there, what?"

The sweet, hungry look in her eyes was just what he'd hoped for. She wanted him as much as he wanted her. For now, anyway. Eager to taste her, he lowered his head.

But instead of initiating the kiss they both wanted, he blurted out the truth.

"Looks as if I'll have to sell Island Air."

LIZA KNEW HER MOUTH was hanging open. She shut it. "Sell Island Air?"

"Afraid so."

D.J.'s arm was no longer around her shoulders. His hands were balled into fists at his sides and his gaze was fixed on the water. The kiss she'd craved and expected since he'd sat down beside her wasn't going to happen. Well, it was safer this way. But frustrating.

"You've probably had enough of my company, huh?" He pushed himself to his feet and offered her a hand. "Come on, I'll take you back."

Clearly, he was upset. Liza took his hand but shook her head. "I'm not ready to leave. I want to know more. I thought you loved airplanes." She tugged on his arm, and he let her pull him down again.

"I do." He let go of her. "Island Air means everything to me."

"Then why—"

"There isn't much else I can do." Arms resting on his knees, he stared into the distance. As if he couldn't or didn't dare to meet her eyes.

Tension radiated from him, so intense she could feel it. Even though he wouldn't look her in the eyes, she could see the anguished set of his jaw. He was in pain. Wanting to ease his distress, she touched his taut cheek. "I'm sorry, D.J."

He jerked his head away. "I don't want your pity."

All right, then. What *did* he want? Questions filled Liza's head, but some sixth sense kept her silent. Which turned out to be the right thing to do, for almost immediately he began to talk.

"You know about my former partner and my ex, right?" he said, fiddling with the twist-off cap on his pop. Liza nodded, and he continued. "They left me in credit hell. Bills you wouldn't believe. I'm still not out from under all the debt. In the fall and winter, the seaplane business slows way down. I missed some payments and now my credit is lousy. There's a big loan due the middle of August. I can't pay it, and the bank won't extend my credit." He rubbed his hand over his face, then at last looked at her. "I can't believe I just told you all that."

"I'm glad you did." Bad enough that his wife and his business partner had walked out on him. But saddling him with their debts, too? Liza bristled with indignation. "Correct me if I'm wrong, but isn't this a community-property state?"

D.J. nodded.

"Then why should you be stuck with your ex-wife's bills? She ought to be responsible for at least part of the debt. If your divorce attorney never mentioned that, you should ask for a refund."

"He did, and so did my accountant. But I just wanted the whole mess behind me." He gave a pained laugh. "Not too swift, huh?"

Her heart ached for him. "You were upset and weren't thinking clearly. I know exactly how that feels."

For a long moment he studied her, his eyes narrowed a fraction. "I guess you do."

Why he looked grateful was beyond her, but his whole face conveyed the message that he was. Liza had never seen a more attractive man. She smiled into his eyes. And just like that, they were back where they'd been earlier, before he'd shared his depressing news.

Only now, her heart was filled with a sense of warmth and caring, and the feeling frightened her. *He doesn't want a relationship. Protect yourself!* warned a voice in her head.

Powerless to move away, she volunteered feebly, "That's what friends do—help each other. Keep me posted?"

"Will do."

Holding her with his gaze, he took a lock of her hair between his fingers and played with it. It was just her hair, for goodness' sake. Yet her insides melted and she really, really wanted him to kiss her.

As if he'd read her mind, his eyes darkened and the air suddenly seemed charged and potent with awareness. He dropped her hair and cupped her face in his hands.

"I don't feel like a friend right now," he said, his voice low and seductive.

"I know."

She leaned forward and kissed him.

D.J.'S BUSINESS PROBLEMS hadn't dampened Liza's interest in him, and for him that was a real turn-on. Her lips were open and soft and yielding, and she tasted of pop and all the warmth of a summer day. Holding her felt good. Too good.

Yes, he'd wanted to kiss her ever since he'd picked her up. And yeah, the plan had been to do just what they were doing. But it wasn't smart, and he should stop. Now.

Instead, he slid his tongue into her willing mouth. She did the same to him. She was eager and responsive, and he knew she'd be a passionate lover. She scooted onto his lap. His body caught fire and he forgot about everything but the woman in his arms.

Her soft buttocks wriggled against his erection, making him so hot, he almost lost control.

"Easy…" He lifted her hips.

"Sorry." She turned in his arms and straddled him, her thighs cradling his hips. "Is this better?"

Her lips found his again, and her warmth pressed hard against his need. It was excruciating—and exquisite.

Desperate to touch her he slipped his hands under the hem of her blouse. He went straight for her breasts, cupping and kneading them gently through her bra. She made a sound of pleasure. Head back, eyes closed, she pushed herself farther into his palms.

So damned sexy. Blood roared in his head. More, he needed more. He wanted her naked and ready for him.

They broke apart at the same time. Breathing hard, Liza unbuttoned her blouse and slipped it off. While D.J. pulled his T-shirt over his head, Liza unhooked the front clasp of her bra. Her breasts spilled out, full and rosy-tipped.

"Beautiful," he murmured. He had to pleasure her. Lowering his head, he slowly and thoroughly laved one taut nipple, loving every taste. He felt her shiver, and stopped. "Cold?"

Her chest, neck and face were flushed with desire. For him.

"Not at all," she said. "I—it feels very good."

"For me, too."

He savored her other breast until he was nearly wild with the breathy catch he heard in her throat and the taste of her skin. Bunching his shirt as a pillow, he gently eased her back on it. Her stomach was pale and smooth. He was unfastening the button on her jeans, when a ferry hooted in the distance.

Liza opened her eyes and looked at him with need and hunger. And a tenderness that terrified him.

She liked him. A lot. And he wasn't ready for that, might never be.

He dropped his arms and sat back on his heels at once. "We shouldn't be doing this."

"You're right." Dazed, her face flushed, she covered herself with her hands and sat up.

His body hard and throbbing, he retrieved her bra and blouse and handed them to her. She turned away from him to put them on. Cursing himself, he tugged on his own shirt and smelled the perfume scent of her hair on it. Damn.

He hadn't meant to let things go so far. But then, the second Liza had touched her lips to his he'd stopped thinking about anything else. She didn't look at him as if he were a loser, and that meant a lot. A whole lot. *She* meant…

Uh-uh. Do not go there. Scared for a totally different reason, he frowned at his straining zipper. Glanced at Liza and caught her staring, too.

She blushed. "I'm not usually like this. I don't just let any man have his way with me."

At the very thought of Liza with some other man, D.J. scowled. "I sure as hell hope not. It's about time for me to go to work." He scooped up the pop bottles and caps and grease-stained food containers and stuffed them into the lunch sack. "I'll take you home."

Within minutes they were back on the bike, flying toward town. Liza didn't hold on to him quite as tightly as before, her grasp more tentative now. Her breasts barely touched his back, and he knew she was holding herself away.

Neither of them spoke again until D.J. signaled and slowed to pull in to her grandma's street.

"I can't go back there, not yet," Liza said. "Let me off here."

At the moment there wasn't much traffic. D.J. eased onto the dirt edge of the road and braked to a stop. Liza slid backward and got off the seat. Biting her lip, she handed him her helmet. She left the sunglasses on. D.J. couldn't see her eyes.

"I can't seem to think rationally around you," she said, continuing the conversation they'd started over lunch.

"Tell me about it." Acutely uncomfortable, he shifted on the bike. "I meant what I said before. I'm not interested in anything serious."

"So you keep saying. But what we did today seemed pretty serious to me."

Seriously dangerous. "Don't get me wrong, I totally

enjoyed that. I just don't want you getting the wrong idea."
He looked her straight in the eye so she'd pay special attention to what he was about to say. "I don't want to hurt you."

"I'm a big girl, D.J., and I have no intention of letting
that happen."

He didn't believe her—not after he'd seen that soft I'm-
falling-for-you look in her eyes. It wasn't there now, though.

"But I do want more than sex," she said. "Since you
clearly don't, I think it'd be best for both of us to not see
each other again."

In full agreement, he nodded.

Call him a fool, but he wanted to kiss her one last time.
Instead, he squeezed the handlebars of the bike and took off.

But riding toward Island Air, he missed the feel of her
at his back. And he knew that staying away from her wasn't
going to be easy.

Chapter Nine

By Friday, Liza had filled the cracks and sanded and primed the walls in the upstairs bedroom. She'd also helped her grandmother sort through some of the numerous boxes that now filled half the living room. By keeping busy every second, she hoped not to think about D.J. But nothing could stem the restless need he'd awakened in her body. It had been two days, but, oh, how she remembered his hands and his fevered mouth on her! Her body tingled and ached, and foolhardy as it was, she wanted more. Much more.

Thank goodness he'd stopped when he did. If he hadn't, she'd have made love with him. Her feelings had been that intense. But then where would she have been? Probably not much worse off than she was now. Want to or not, she was falling in love with the man, and he didn't even want a girlfriend. Let alone love.

Where was her common sense when she needed it?

The one saving grace was that D.J. didn't know. At least she still had her dignity.

Gram had been wonderful. One look at Liza, when she'd

at last returned from those passionate few hours, and she'd frowned. "Why, Liza, you're upset. What's happened?"

"Everything's fine, Gram." Liza had mustered a cheerful expression.

Her grandmother's skeptical look made it clear that she didn't believe that, but she'd left Liza alone. So different from Diane, who would have pushed and prodded. Which was why Liza had dawdled, walking up Clam Digger Way, both to compose herself and to give her mother time to leave.

"Thanks for not prying," she'd said at dinner.

"Doesn't mean I'm not concerned. Whatever happened, if you want to talk, I'm here," her grandmother had replied.

"I know, and I appreciate that."

Later that evening, Diane had called for an "update," her voice all singsong and warm. Liza had repeated that she and D.J. were friends. Even if they weren't anymore.

Liza could hardly wait to go to Tina's for dinner that evening. Surely a few hours with her old friend and her family would distract Liza from thoughts of D.J.

On the way out she kissed Gram's powdery soft cheek. "Sure you don't mind me going?"

In the process of making herself a salad, Gram paused. "The past few days you've done nothing but work. You need to have fun with people your own age. So please go and enjoy yourself."

"Thanks, Gram. I love you."

"You, too, honey. Did I mention that I'm playing bridge with G.G. and the girls next week?" G.G. was the kind, elderly woman who had raised Tina and who lived across the street from her now. She and Gram had played cards together for decades, and Gram always enjoyed herself.

"You'll be here alone that night," her grandmother said. "Will you mind?"

"Not at all. I'm glad *you're* getting out, too. By the way, there's a teaching job open in Seattle. I applied for it this morning."

"Oh." Gram sighed. "I guess you've made up your mind about this house."

"You know I'd love to live in it." Liza meant that. Living close to her grandmother in this special home on the island would be wonderful. On the other hand, D.J. and her mother were here, too. And then there was the minor matter of an income. "I need a teaching job, Gram. Believe me, if the Halo Island School District had something…"

Though in truth, it was almost a relief that there were no openings here.

"I know, honey. It's not your fault." Gram looked out the window at the view she'd enjoyed for the past fifty-four years. "I suppose I should call a Realtor."

Liza wasn't ready for that. Yet she couldn't live here, either. Talk about confused! She shook her head. "Not just yet. First, let me finish the upstairs."

"All right. Why don't you take Tina some flowers from the garden."

"That's a nice idea. I will."

Twenty minutes later, Liza pulled up in front of Tina and Ryan Chase's house, which was located on Huckleberry Hill Road, a charming dead-end street in the middle of the island.

She hadn't been here in ages. Carrying the fragrant, colorful bouquet she'd snipped from Gram's garden, and a bottle of wine from the grocery store, she knocked on the screen door.

"Hi, Liza." A smiling Tina opened the door and Liza walked into the warm, friendly home. "Ryan and Maggie went to the store for ice cream for dessert tonight. They'll be back shortly. These are gorgeous flowers—I love roses and sweet peas. And dahlias, too." She sniffed the blossoms. "What a sweet smell. Come into the kitchen while I find a vase."

"This is a great house," Liza said as they passed the ample living room and dining room and entered the cheerful kitchen.

"Thanks. Ryan bought it before we knew each other. It's a good thing, too. If he hadn't moved into the neighborhood, we'd never have met."

She was positively glowing. "You look fantastic," Liza said. "Tell me your secret."

"The love of a good man and a sweet little girl. I've never been happier." Tina told Liza about Ryan, a widower and banker who had moved to Halo Island with his young daughter several years earlier. Since then, he'd bought Halo Island Bank. "Who would've believed I'd fall in love with a man who lived across the street from the house where I grew up?"

"That *is* amazing. What's it like, living so close to G.G.?"

"It's the best. I can check on her anytime, and if she needs help, all I have to do is run over. That gives us all peace of mind."

Which was a solid reason for Liza to move into Gram's house. Especially with Diane and Art traveling so much. "My grandmother wants me to move into her house," she told Tina.

"That'd be great. Then we could see each other more

than once every few years. You could join our monthly bunco game, which we just started at the community center—we need players. Why don't we sit out back, where it's shady and cool. I'll open your wine, too, and bring out some nibblies. We're grilling steaks tonight, but I don't want to light the charcoal until Ryan and Maggie get back."

"That sounds perfect," Liza said.

They took the bottle, glasses and a plate of snacks out onto the lawn. Flowers rimmed the border and several leafy trees shaded the patio. In one corner stood a swing set and a small playhouse, a little girl's paradise.

"How is it, being a mom?" Liza asked as they settled into comfortable deck chairs.

"Better than I'd ever imagined. Wait'll you meet Maggie." Tina smiled. "She's the most wonderful child. I love her like my very own."

Liza was eager to meet Maggie and Ryan. "Last time I saw you, you were off to college. I kept hearing stories about you, working your way to the top of that marketing company in Seattle. Then I met your friend, Kendra, when I flew over, and she tells me *she* has the job you gave up, and that you helped her get it."

"That's right. I never thought I'd fall in love or choose to quit my job, but I did. I am still working part-time, though. I handle the advertising and marketing for Halo Island Bank."

"How does Ryan like owning the bank?"

"Loves it. He's such a terrific guy." She had a dreamy look on her face. "We're so lucky we found each other."

Liza envied her. "Do you ever have regrets and wish you had your job back?"

"The long days and all that stress?" Tina laughed. "No way. I was tired of working there before I met Ryan. He helped me see that." She leaned forward. "You were going to tell me about your grandmother's house. I heard that she was moving into the Sunset."

"That's why I'm on the island, to help with the packing and moving. She's downsizing from a three-bedroom, two-bathroom house to a one-bedroom, one-bathroom apartment. Talk about a huge change."

Tina made a face. "I can't even imagine."

"Gram seems ready to move, so that makes the whole thing easier. Her heart isn't so good, and I think living in a one-story apartment, with people to look in on her and a dining room where she can get her meals if she doesn't feel like cooking, will be great. But taking apart the house and deciding what to keep and what to let go… That's rough. There are lots of memories there."

"G.G.'s house is like that, filled with all sorts of treasures that mean something to her. And to me. I don't even want to think about how it will be if she ever decides to move." Tina shuddered. "You said your grandmother offered you the house? That's incredibly generous."

Liza nodded. "I still can't believe it, but she did."

"It'd be so great if you lived here. But I suppose you have a teaching job to get back to."

"I was laid off," Liza said. At Tina's sympathetic look, she shrugged. "I'll find something."

"Have you checked the school district here?"

"Every morning."

"Last year the third-grade teacher got married. I happen to know that she wants to have a baby, quit her job and be a full-time mom. It hasn't happened yet, but they're trying."

That could take a while. And the woman might decide to keep her job, after all. "I can't afford to wait."

"You could be a tutor or open a preschool."

"Those are possibilities," Liza said. "But I need a regular full-time salary, and I really want to teach." She bit her lip. "Actually, this morning I applied for a job in Seattle."

"A girl's gotta do what she must. But trust me, it'd be a whole lot easier for you and D.J. if you lived here."

Liza nearly choked on her wine. "What are you talking about?"

"Aren't you two involved?"

They definitely had been—for one romantic sunset and one extremely titillating afternoon, but as far as Liza knew, no one but she and D.J. was aware of either of those. "We're hardly even friends," she said.

Not anymore. Being friends with D.J. was way too dangerous.

"Oh. I thought…" Tina looked surprised. "The other night at the Gull's Nest you looked like a couple. I could almost see the electricity between you. And I heard that you were on the back of D.J.'s Harley the other day, holding on tight when you stopped at Clams. I imagine D.J. is pretty nice to hold on to." Tina's eyebrows rose dramatically.

So, maybe people knew about their lunch from Clams. Liza recalled how exciting it had been to ride behind that big, sexy male, pressed against his hard back. Smelling his aftershave and feeling those powerful muscles work as he handled the Harley. For a moment her insides went soft. But she was over all that now.

"That was just lunch," she said. "There really is nothing between us."

"What a shame, because D.J.'s a cool guy and a great pilot, with a wry sense of humor. It's a shame about Island Air."

Liza wasn't surprised that Tina knew about that. Probably by now everyone on the island did. "I know. He really loves that company."

"Has he talked to Ryan? My husband doesn't tell me what goes on with his clients—it's confidential. But if D.J. hasn't made an appointment, he should."

"I think so," Liza said. Wanting to push the man from her thoughts, she changed the subject. "Catch me up on the other people from our school."

Tina was in the process of doing just that when they heard the sound of a car pulling in to the driveway.

"Ryan and Maggie are back." She grinned and jumped up. "Come on."

Hours later, sated from a delicious meal, laughter and good conversation, Liza stood at Tina and Ryan's front door. "I had a wonderful time," she told them.

"It's always good to meet Tina's friends," Ryan said, slipping his arm around his wife. "Come back anytime."

He was handsome and friendly, and clearly crazy about Tina. She adored him, too. They seemed perfect for each other, sharing the kind of love Liza had always dreamed of but still hadn't found.

Standing between Ryan and Tina, redheaded Maggie grinned, revealing an adorable dimple and two missing front teeth. "I like you, Liza. You're fun."

Liza's heart melted. "I like you, too, Maggie. Thank you

for sharing your parents and your dinner with me. And for introducing me to your hamster." Who was imaginatively named Eggwhite.

Maggie beamed. "She says to come back and play again soon."

"Come visit anytime," Tina said. "Keep me posted on the job. I'll keep my ears open for you."

"Thanks."

As pleasant as the evening had been, on the drive home, Liza couldn't help comparing her life with Tina's and coming up short. She longed for what her friend had, so much so that her heart ached.

But the answer certainly wasn't D.J. Hatcher. He didn't want to get serious. Liza did. She wanted the dream— love, marriage and kids. Soon. Why had she wasted three years moping over Timothy?

As she pulled onto Clam Digger Way, she made a vow. It was time to find a man who was looking for the same things. Once she found a job and moved, that would be the priority.

ON D.J.'s LAST FLIGHT late Sunday afternoon, with a plane full of passengers, he prepared to land on Halo Island. The sky was blue, the water sparkled, and as always, everyone on board was slightly dazzled. They were eager to land and so was D.J. But as he began the descent, instead of aiming straight for his landing spot, he changed course, turned toward the opposite end of the island and headed for Mrs. Haverford's house.

"Thought I'd give you folks a quick peek at the island before we land," he said. Which sounded logical to him.

Liza and her grandma were in the backyard. At two

hundred feet above them, he was close enough to see the older woman wave. D.J. saluted. He couldn't see their faces, but he figured they were surprised. And maybe impressed.

D.J. imagined Liza looking at him as she had the other day, when she lay bare breasted on the rock. No judgment in her expression, only a sweet tenderness. Okay, that had scared him spitless, but at the time he hadn't realized how badly he needed her approval.

It had been four days since that incredible afternoon, and he knew it now. He still wanted her, so much that a certain part of his body was constantly half aroused. More than sex, he needed her assurance and acceptance, the way an addict needed a fix.

Which was just plain crazy. And exactly why he wouldn't be seeing her again.

He circled back. "I know you're anxious to be on your way, so I'll head for the dock now. We'll be touching down in roughly five minutes."

The landing was smooth and uneventful. Once the plane emptied, D.J. cleaned up the cabin and readied it for tomorrow. Then he headed for the office. At this hour, the reservations desk was closed and the place was empty. No incriminating stares or muttered comments to make him feel worse than he already did.

When he got to his desk, he called Liza's grandmother to see how she'd liked his visit.

"Hello," Liza said.

At the sound of her voice D.J.'s heart tripped over itself. "Hey there. Did you see me salute?"

"Yes. Why'd you fly over the house like that? It was noisy and windy, and you about gave Gram a heart attack."

So she wasn't thrilled. Yet D.J. couldn't help but grin. He paced to the window and looked out, watching the gulls wheel lazily over the water. Damn, it was good to talk to her. "I think she liked it. She waved. Admit it, Liza. You liked it, too."

He heard her sigh. "It was awfully loud."

"If it really bothers you, maybe you should come over here and we'll discuss it," he said, forgetting that he didn't want to see her.

"Don't you remember what we both decided? We aren't going to be around each other."

True. Disappointed, D.J. sank onto his desk chair. "Okay, scratch the invite. Let me talk to your grandma."

"What for?"

"To apologize."

"All right." Her hand muffled the receiver, but D.J. heard her raise her voice. "He wants to talk to you, Gram."

A good fifteen seconds later, her grandmother spoke. "Hello, D.J."

She sounded out of breath. D.J. wondered if she'd run to the phone. "Hi, Mrs. H. Didn't mean to upset you when I flew over earlier."

"Wherever did you get that idea? I thought it was exciting."

D.J. was pleased to hear that. "That's exactly what I told Liza."

"Good for you." Her grandma chuckled. "Say, D.J., why don't you come for dinner, Wednesday night? We'll grill fresh salmon and I'll bake you a homemade strawberry pie."

His mouth watered. Over the phone he heard a noise that sounded an awful lot like Liza groaning, and not in a good way.

"I don't think Liza wants me there." For both their sakes, he should turn down this invitation.

"Nonsense. She would love your company," her grandma said in a firm voice that nobody, not even Liza, was likely to argue with. "Diane and Art also will be here with their vacation brochures, and I know Liza would appreciate your company. Wouldn't you, dear?"

During the brief pause D.J. pictured Liza rolling her eyes. Then he heard her say, "Give me back the phone, Gram."

"Liza wants to talk to you. Goodbye, D.J. We'll be sitting down at seven, so come any time before that. Maybe after dinner, you and Liza can head down to the beach for the sunset."

Another sunset with Liza—exactly what D.J. did not need. But he *wanted* it. He was also interested in a home-cooked dinner and that pie. "Thanks, Mrs. H. I'll be there."

Then, Liza took the phone. "You don't have to come," she said.

"I told your grandma I would. She's making my favorite pie. Besides, with your mom and stepfather there, you might need me."

Liza took a moment to process the thought. "You're right. Anything new with Island Air?"

"The Realtor will be here next week to list it."

Thinking about that hurt like a knife in the chest.

"So you're selling. I'm sorry, D.J."

"Yeah." Part of him hoped that once the property went on the market, it would sell fast, like ripping a Band-Aid off a recent wound and being done with it. A larger part of him hoped that it never sold. But that meant foreclosure, which was even worse. Both choices were terrible. A headache was developing behind his eyes. D.J. massaged the space above his nose.

"Have you talked with Ryan Chase at Halo Island Bank? I met him the other night, at Tina's. He's wonderful."

"We talked a few weeks back. He can't help me. How's your job search going?"

"There's an opening in Seattle. I've applied for it."

D.J. wished there was something on Halo Island, so she could stay. A thought that had him scowling. For her grandma's sake, he assured himself, not for him. Once the business sold, he was out of here, anyway. "I'm sure they'll hire you," he said.

"We'll see. I have to make it through the interview process first."

"When is that?"

"I only applied on Friday. They haven't called yet."

"They will." He wondered whether he'd be the one to fly her to Seattle.

"I should go. Goodbye, D.J."

He hung up feeling better than he had any right to. Swore silently and decided to skip the paperwork and go for a run. It had been a while, and the exercise should clear his head.

He would not think about Liza Miller anymore tonight. Or tomorrow. Or any time at all. But even as he silently vowed to forget her, he looked forward to seeing her Wednesday night.

Chapter Ten

Just before six-thirty Wednesday night, Liza set the cloth napkins around the dining-room table where Gram wanted to eat. Because of their "special" dinner company, she said.

"Special" meaning Diane and Art. And D.J.

Liza hoped her mother behaved tonight. Since D.J. was a guest, she probably would. There was another, bigger concern—her own feelings for D.J. She liked him way too much. Of course, no one else knew that, and no one ever would. On the other hand, since she firmly intended to move past this ridiculous crush on the man, there was nothing to worry about. She had it all planned. Starting tonight, she would distance herself from him, and by the time she started a new job he would be completely out of her system. Then she'd be primed and ready to find the right person for her, a man who wanted love and marriage and children. It was a good strategy, and simply repeating it eased her anxieties about the evening ahead.

It was also the reason she was wearing a dress she'd brought with her from Bellingham, a loose cream-colored shift as modest as a nun's habit. Dressed this way, she felt safe. Plus, by wearing this outfit, she would let both Gram and her mother know that she really wasn't interested in attracting D.J.'s attention.

Never mind that he already knew what her breasts looked like. The heaven of his mouth, his tongue against her sensitive nipples... Even now they swelled and ached for his ministrations. Liza swallowed.

Stop that. Lips compressed, she finished setting the table.

"Look at these flowers from the garden," Gram said as she entered the room with a brimming vase. "Don't they make a colorful centerpiece?" She set the sweet-smelling arrangement in the middle of the table. "I only picked red, pink and white—the colors of love and romance."

Liza groaned. "There *is* no romance, and certainly no love, between D.J. and me," she stated for what seemed like the twelfth time.

"Well, your mother and Art will appreciate the gesture. Their anniversary is a week from today, you know."

July second, which also was the day they left for Australia. "Fine, but D.J. and I will look at them as nothing more than pretty table flowers."

Her grandmother's calculating expression worried Liza. Why oh why hadn't she talked D.J. into staying away? "Please, please, please, don't try to push us together tonight."

"I'd never do that," her grandmother said, looking offended. Seconds later, she eyed Liza. "Are you sure you want to wear that dress? There's still time to change your clothes."

"I'm sure. You worked hard this afternoon. Why don't you sit down in the living room and relax."

"I will, if you'll turn on the oven for the potato casserole and put out the salad."

Liza set the oven. Then she carried Gram's large wooden salad bowl to the table and renewed her resolve. No matter what her grandmother or mother did or said, she intended to sail through the evening. As if D.J. were nothing but a casual dinner guest. Come tomorrow, this whole "crush" business would be behind her.

"I just heard a motorcycle," Gram called from the living room.

Liza's heart fluttered annoyingly. Hardly aware of her actions she fluffed her hair and smoothed her dress. And stayed in the kitchen.

The doorbell rang. "I'm on my way to the bathroom," Gram said. "You'll have to get that."

"All right." Forcing herself to walk slowly, Liza headed for the door and opened it.

D.J. stood there, looking every bit as good in a dress shirt and slacks as he did in a T-shirt and jeans.

"Hello, D.J."

"Hey, there."

His gaze flitted over her, dark and appreciative, despite her unrevealing dress. Responding warmth flooded her, and for a moment she almost forgot to breathe.

"These are for you and your grandma." He thrust a bottle of wine and a bouquet of grocery-store carnations at her.

"Thank you."

"Are you going to invite me in?"

Clutching the gifts, she pushed the door open wider. "Diane and Art aren't here yet. Have a seat in the living room and make yourself comfortable. Shall I open this wine?"

"It's for dinner. How about a beer?"

"I'll get it, and I'll put these in a vase." Liza was about to head for the kitchen, when Gram returned from the bathroom. "D.J. brought these flowers for you," she said. "And a nice bottle of wine."

"My. Thank you, D.J. The wine will go perfectly with our salmon. You can put the flowers in the dining room, Liza."

D.J. looked past them at the vase of garden flowers, and scratched the back of his neck. "You didn't really need store-bought flowers, did you?"

"You put that thought right out of your head," Liza's grandmother said. "The house can always use more flowers. You're sweet to bring them. Thoughtful."

To Liza's surprise, D.J. blushed. For such an attractive man, he wasn't at all arrogant. This made her like him even more. Which caused her to frown. At this rate, she'd never get over him.

"Diane and Art should be here any minute," Gram said. "Why don't you start the coals, Liza. D.J. can help you, and I'll prepare the green beans."

Liza didn't need help, but she did want to warn D.J. about the evening ahead. "Okay."

As she took D.J. down a short hallway that led to the back door, she could feel his gaze on her. In her dress, there wasn't much to see. When they stepped onto the back stoop, he gave the flower garden an admiring glance.

"Wow," he said, stepping onto the patio. "With all the trees and the high fence, this is like your own private park. Great yard, great location, great house, period. No wonder you're torn about leaving it."

It wasn't a topic she wanted to discuss tonight. "Gram

has a green thumb. Or at least she did. She's mostly given up gardening. My mother took over the job for a while. Now I'm doing it. But I'm not as talented. Growing things never has been my forte."

Why was she telling D.J. this? He couldn't possibly care. She strode toward the grill. "I need to warn you about my grandmother."

D.J. followed her. "She likes me," he said with a charming, crooked smile.

Suddenly Liza could picture him as an adorable young boy, getting whatever he wanted with that irresistible grin. At the moment, *she'd* certainly give him whatever he asked for. Ideally, something that had to do with kissing and pleasure… With grim determination she halted that train of thought.

"She's a hopeless romantic. No matter what I say, she seems to think there's something between us, when we both know there isn't."

"Oh yes there is." D.J.'s voice was low and intimate. "A red-hot sexual connection that's making me crazy." He glanced at her mouth with unveiled lust.

Her traitorous body began to hum, and even knowing that Gram was in the house and Diane and Art would soon arrive, Liza wanted to push D.J. onto the grass, kiss him and more, and to heck with getting hurt. It was all she could do to keep from pulling him closer.

Frightened by her reckless feelings, she grabbed the bag of charcoal and poured a healthy amount into the top of the brazier, a metal cylinder that would heat the coals without requiring lighter fluid. "We're supposed to be putting that behind us, remember?"

"I'm trying, but I'm not having much luck." D.J. advanced toward her. "I don't think you are, either."

Was she that easy to read? Liza backed away. "It doesn't help when you look at me that way."

"What way?" he asked, his eyes hungry with desire.

As if he hadn't eaten in days and she was something delicious. "Like you want me. You're doing it now, D.J."

"Am I?" Swearing, he glanced away. "I shouldn't have come. But your grandma invited me. She made a pie. What was I supposed to do, lie and say I was busy?"

"Yes."

"But your mom will be here. You need me."

Since it was likely that his mere presence would temper Diane's behavior, that was true. Still… "You never know what Diane might do or say, so let me apologize up front for anything that happens."

"Thanks for the warning. If you need any help from me, touch your finger to your nose, like so…" He put his index finger to the tip of his nose. "And I'll jump in and save you."

Relieved that they'd moved to a less dangerous subject, Liza laughed. "My hero. Thanks, D.J. Now, if we want to convince my mother and Gram that we're only friends, no more of those looks."

"Hot looks over and done with. You got it. We'd better fire up the grill or your grandma will wonder what we're doing out here." Mouth quirking, D.J. held out his palm. "Hand over the matches."

He struck one, then touched it to the wadded-up newspaper that Liza had packed into the bottom of the brazier. The flame caught and spread, quickly engulfing the paper.

Similar to the way her attraction to D.J. burned through her common sense.

What in the world had led her to believe she could quickly get over him?

She would, however, and no excuses. Starting now. Liza turned toward the door. "It's time to go inside and keep Gram company."

"WOULD YOU LIKE another beer?" Liza's grandma asked, smiling at D.J.

She really did seem to like him. He liked her, too.

They were in the living room, seated in matching chairs that faced the big window with its ocean view. Liza's grandma sat on the sofa, looking at the two of them instead of the water. It was pretty obvious that she wanted D.J. to become involved with Liza. D.J. wanted that, too, only his fantasies involved no clothes and lots of incredible sex. Probably not exactly what Mrs. Haverford was imagining.

He shook his head. "I'm good, thanks."

Liza's mom and stepdad weren't here yet, and as the minutes dragged by he began to wish he hadn't come. At the same time he was exactly where he wanted to be. Talk about confusing. Even more confusing, he would've killed for Liza to gaze at him again with that special tender expression that he couldn't erase from his memory.

Not gonna happen tonight. Aside from a few brief, warm looks outside, she'd barely glanced at him. He realized that he'd mistaken genuine feelings of friendship for sexual arousal. Apparently, she really meant what she said—beyond sexual attraction, there was nothing between them.

Which was great, right? If he felt empty, it was simply because he hadn't eaten in hours. He glanced at his watch and Mrs. Haverford frowned.

"I can't imagine what's keeping Diane and Art," she said. "They're always so punctual. I'm beginning to worry."

"Mother probably decided to change her outfit at the last minute. I'm sure they'll be here soon."

Both females were quiet then, Mrs. Haverford looking anxious and Liza tapping her fingers against the arm of her chair.

Just as uncomfortable, D.J. shifted in his seat. It was going to be a long night. At last, he thought of something to talk about. "Say, Mrs. H., do you need help moving? If so, I have a pickup truck. I'm available nights and any Saturday."

Now, why in the world had he offered to help her? He should've kept his mouth shut.

Liza shot him a distressed look. "You don't have to do that, D.J."

But her grandma smiled. "How sweet. It just so happens, I'm scheduled to move on the second Saturday in July."

"I'll be here."

"You're a darling. I like you, and I like Island Air. Isn't there some way to change your mind about selling?"

Apparently, Liza's grandma didn't know about his financial troubles. "It's already on the market," he said.

"What'll you do after you sell?"

"Find something else."

"Will you be staying on the island?"

"Gram, stop pestering him with questions."

D.J. didn't mind. Now was as good a time as any to share his plans. "I'll be moving, but I don't know exactly where."

Liza looked shocked at this. "You are? Why didn't you tell me?"

"I just did."

Mrs. Haverford's phone rang, cutting short the discussion.

"I'll bet that's my mother." Liza stood and hurried into the kitchen to answer the call.

In the living room, it was easy to hear her end of the conversation, and D.J. and her grandma listened openly.

"Oh, Mother, I'm so sorry," Liza said. "Do you want me to come over?"

Her grandma shot D.J. a confused look. He shrugged.

She hung up and came back into the room shaking her head. "Mother and Art won't be here, after all," she said. "They were almost out the door, when Art threw up. Then Mother did, too. Neither of them can leave the bathroom. They think it's food poisoning—something they ate at lunch."

"Oh, my," Mrs. Haverford said. "That's terrible."

Liza bit her lip. "I offered to come over and check on them." She glanced at D.J. "I always used to take care of my mother when she was sick, even when my father was alive. She used to like that. This time, she said she didn't need me, that I should stay here."

"You're going over there anyway, right?" D.J. said.

"Do you think I should?"

"Heck, yes. What if they need to go to the hospital or something? Forget dinner and go."

"It certainly would ease my mind," Mrs. Haverford said. "I'd go with you, but I'm sure they don't want both of us around." She looked at D.J. "I'm sorry about this. Can we try again tomorrow night? I'm leaving to play bridge at seven, but you could come at six. The salmon won't be quite as fresh, but it'll still be good. We'll save the pie, too."

D.J. wanted that meal. But afterward Mrs. Haverford would take off, leaving him and Liza alone. Not a good idea—downright dangerous. But he saw that the older woman wanted him to come back. Torn, he looked to Liza. She seemed equally undecided.

"Why don't you and Liza talk it over when she walks you out," her grandma said. "While you do that, Liza, I'll make you a quick sandwich to eat on the way to your mother's. I'll rustle up some cola, too, for their upset stomachs."

As D.J. followed Liza out the front door, his eyes settled on her behind. In that sacklike dress, he couldn't see more than a hint of her shape, but it was still enough to stir him up.

They headed across the front yard. "You weren't kidding about your grandma," he said close to her ear so the older woman couldn't hear. "She really does want us to get together."

He caught a whiff of perfume and woman, and quickly drew back. But it was too late. The fierce need he'd battled all evening—hell, for days—surged through him. "So do I," he growled.

Unable to stop himself, he caught Liza's hands and pulled her to the backside of the garage, out of sight from anyone except the squirrels in the bushes. Legs splayed, leaning against the cool siding, he pulled Liza between his thighs and kissed her.

The hunger he tasted on her mouth fueled his own desire. His body went hard. He grasped her soft behind and pulled her tight against his arousal, so that she could feel what she did to him. When he broke the kiss, he cupped her face so that she would look at him. "I want you badly, Liza, and you want me just as much."

He heard her swallow, saw the stark need in her face, and it was all he could do to keep from finishing what they'd started right then, against the garage siding. But Liza deserved better.

"There's only one way to get past this thing between us, and you know what it is," he said, looking into those big eyes. "If I come back tomorrow night, it won't be for the salmon or the pie. It'll be to make love with you. And when I do, it'll be slow and thorough." Of its own accord, his thumb stroked the rapid pulse under her chin. "If you don't want that, say it now."

"I do," she replied without a moment's hesitation.

He kissed her again, a quick but promise-filled taste of what was to come. When he released her, his body felt as if it might explode and his hands were shaking.

"Tell your grandma I'll be here at six."

TEN MINUTES AFTER D.J.'s searing kiss, her lips still tingling, Liza parked Gram's car in her mother and Art's driveway. Beside her, the sandwich Gram had made lay untouched in its plastic bag. After what had happened with D.J. tonight and knowing what was to come, who could eat?

Against her better judgment, she was going to make love with D.J. Slow and thorough, he'd said. Oh, how she wanted and needed that, and she thought she could hardly bear the twenty-four-hour wait. She fervently hoped that what he said was true, that once they made love they'd be free of each other. Then, she could get on with her life. So could he.

But now was no time to think about D.J. or tomorrow night. Art and her mother were sick and needed her. In the still-bright sunlight, carrying two large bottles of cola, Liza strode through the arched walkway that led to the house where she'd lived for the first sixteen years of her life.

She hadn't been here in three years, and it felt slightly uncomfortable now. And she wasn't even inside yet.

Like her grandmother's place, this house, too, faced the beach. Painted a tasteful cream with dark green shutters, it was as carefully maintained and tidy as Diane was. The small garden beneath the window was planted with dahlias of all kinds, which surely impressed the garden-club ladies.

Liza walked up the brick walkway, lifted the brass knocker and knocked.

No answer. She tried the knob, but it was locked. So she rang the doorbell. "It's Liza. Let me in."

Seconds later the latch clicked and the door opened. Wearing a summer robe and matching slippers, looking drawn and ashen, her mother leaned heavily against the frame. "I told you not to come. You're supposed to be at your grandmother's, enjoying grilled salmon with D.J."

"I was too worried about you to eat. Gram sent cola." Liza held up the bottles.

"Thanks. Come on in."

Liza followed her into a spacious living room that was ten times as plush as Gram's but not nearly as warm or cozy. "How's Art?"

"He's in the bathroom, too sick to come out. This past hour has been absolutely horrible. I'm just grateful for more than one toilet." She covered her mouth. "Dear God," she moaned, racing for the powder room.

While she was gone, Liza went into the kitchen to fill two glasses with cola, one for her mother, the other for Art. She carried the drinks into the living room and waited.

For a few moments, the only sounds in the room were the gull's cries through the sliding glass doors that fronted the view and the barely audible click of the pendulum clock on the fireplace mantel.

At last, her mother returned. She flopped heavily onto the sofa, then eyed her cola as if it were poison.

"You don't want to get dehydrated," Liza said. "At least try a sip."

Diane nodded and did as she was told. Just as she always had when she was sick and Liza had mothered her. Mothering her mother. It was the only time Diane had ever seemed to appreciate Liza. Which probably was why Liza had taken on the task at an early age.

"I poured one for Art, too," she said.

"Would you please take it to him?"

Her stepfather was still closeted in the master bathroom. Having no great desire to see him in his pajamas, Liza left his glass on the bedside table and quickly returned to the living room.

Her mother looked exhausted and dull-eyed. "Should I call the doctor or would you like me to take you to the hospital?" Liza asked.

"We're not *that* sick. As a matter of fact, I'm starting to feel better. I think the cola is helping."

"That's great. Since you're better, maybe I should go and let you rest."

"Not yet. I'd love for you to look at the travel brochures. They're on the table in the entry."

Liza retrieved them, then settled herself on a Queen Anne–style chair, its rigid back and hard seat less than inviting. Going through the motions, she leafed through the information. When she turned to ask her mother a question, Diane's eyes were closed.

Now it really was time to leave. Liza stood.

"I'm so sorry Art and I ruined dinner with D.J.," her mother said, her eyes remaining closed.

"That's okay. Gram invited him back tomorrow night."

At this, her mother's lids opened wide. To hide her feelings, Liza rolled her eyes.

"I wish I could be there, but Art and I have a fund-raiser for the garden club. I do hope you'll wear something more attractive than that dress you have on now."

This sounded more like the mother Liza knew and barely tolerated.

"Why bother, when there's nothing between D.J and me?" Except a raging case of mutual sexual attraction. Which they would take care of tomorrow night.

"I heard that he buzzed the house Sunday. If you ask me, he wants more than friendship."

"He wanted to show his passengers a bird's-eye view of the island, that's all."

"Or maybe he wanted to show off for you. If he likes you despite your hair, makeup and clothing, I—"

"You really *are* feeling better. You're criticizing me again. Stop it."

"I only do it because I want the best for you." Diane raised her head off the sofa pillows, in order to take another sip of her drink.

"What you want for me isn't what I want for myself."

Her mother gave her a pained look. "I realize I made a mistake about Timothy."

It was the first time ever she'd acknowledged that she'd been wrong. "You've never said that before," Liza said.

"Well, now I have. Back to D.J. Your grandmother tells me he reads books. He's good-looking and articulate. Word is, he's going to sell his company. I understand there's a loan to pay off, but I suspect that even so, he'll walk away with a tidy sum. You could do worse."

Her mother was giving the relationship with D.J. her blessing. Liza could hardly believe what she was hearing. It was nice—except there was no relationship. "D.J. and I... There's no future."

"Then why is he coming back for dinner tomorrow night?"

"Because Gram invited him." Unable to meet her mother's eyes, Liza smoothed down her skirt.

"Are you sure that's the only reason?" Diane's pale lips smiled. "I think you care for him."

"Only as a friend." Liza tried with all her might to make that so.

"I'm sorry to hear that. But you know best."

Words she'd never expected to hear from her mother's lips. Food poisoning seemed to have softened her. Or possibly it had addled her brain.

"I appreciate your confidence in me," Liza said.

Eyes closed again, Diane nodded. "I think I'll go to sleep now."

"Good idea. You'll call me if you need anything, right?"

"Believe me, I will."

Chapter Eleven

The following afternoon, D.J. handed off his last flight of the day to a sub—something he rarely did, unless company business forced him to. This time was different, though. He was that eager to be with Liza. The best part of the whole arrangement was that she didn't want to get involved any more than he did. They desired each other physically, period.

He was pulling out his aviator sunglasses and striding toward the Harley, when Joe fell into step beside him.

"Got a minute?"

Lately their friendship had been strained. In no mood for a talk that would surely bring him down, D.J. slipped on his shades. "Only a minute." He kept on walking. "Can whatever you want to say keep till tomorrow?"

"I don't think you want to wait on this."

That sounded ominous, and it stopped D.J. cold. Pivoting toward Joe, he braced for something bad. "Go ahead."

"The pilots, the mechanics, Mary and Sue—everybody's been talking about you."

"I'll just bet they have." D.J. imagined all the names they were calling him. *Failure. Loser.* And a few other choice epithets. Hands low on his hips, he eyed Joe. "All right, get it out of your system."

"Huh?" His friend looked confused. "I meant, we've been talking about what to do. We think we know a way for you to hold on to Island Air."

This was a total surprise, and D.J. knew that he was showing it. "How?"

"It's like this. Not counting you, there are seven full-time permanent employees. None of is us rich, but we all have some money saved. We figure if we each chip in, you'll have enough to pay off that loan. In return, you can give us shares in the company."

"We're talking two hundred fifty thousand and some odd dollars."

"We know. Counting our retirement accounts, we can come up with it."

"You can't risk your retirement for Island Air."

"Sure we can. Otherwise, we wouldn't offer. What do you think?"

D.J. wasn't sure *what* to think. "Partners, huh?"

All seven full-timers had worked for D.J. the whole five years. They'd been here through thick and thin, had even endured a couple of late paychecks. They were loyal to the core, and D.J. knew he could trust them. Thing was, he didn't want even one partner, let alone seven.

"We wouldn't have enough of a stake to take over or anything. None of us want the responsibility. Running the business is your job. You could write that into the deal. What we *do* want, is a share of the profits. That's how we'll make back our retirement."

D.J. snorted. "What profits?"

"We believe in Island Air, and we believe in you. Eventually, there will be some."

Then they didn't think D.J. was a failure, after all. Their faith in him was overwhelming. Damned if his eyes didn't tear up. Grateful for his sunglasses, he blinked several times.

"Interesting proposal," he said. And not nearly as risky as taking on one equal partner. The more D.J. thought about the proposal, the more it appealed to him. He was amazed that Joe and the others had come up with the idea. "Let me run it by my accountant and get back to you."

Not that it was Carter's decision, but D.J. respected the man and wanted his advice.

"Sure, Deej."

"Thanks for the suggestion, buddy." He clapped Joe on the shoulder.

Joe flushed. "That's what friends are for."

A GOOD TEN MINUTES before six o'clock, bearing wine, a quart of high-quality vanilla ice cream to go with the strawberry pie, and with two foil packets in his hip pocket, D.J. stood at Liza's grandmother's door.

"Hello, D.J." Opening the screen, Liza tried to smile but failed.

Nervous about later, he guessed. On edge himself, he nodded. "Hey, there." He let his attention wander over her jeans and pretty lemon-yellow shirt. "You look nice tonight." *And I can't wait to get you naked.*

"Thanks. You're earlier then we expected. My grandmother's still getting dressed."

"Yeah? Then, let me say hello in a whole different way." He leaned down for a kiss. A short but sizzling kiss.

When he straightened, Liza looked dazed and flushed.

"You'd better put that ice cream in the freezer," he said.

"Oh. Right."

She turned away and headed for the kitchen. D.J. followed, his attention on her outstanding behind. He wanted to tell her about Joe's employee-partnership idea and see what she thought. But first...

"How're your mom and stepfather doing?" he asked.

"As of lunchtime, they were feeling much better. Which is a good thing, since they have a fund-raiser tonight."

"That's good news. Need any help with dinner?"

"I'm about to toss the salad. Otherwise, everything's ready." *Including me,* her eyes told him.

What that look did to D.J.... He wished her grandmother was on her way already. "Were they glad you stopped by?"

"I didn't see Art, but my mother and I had a mostly decent conversation." Color flooded her cheeks, and she glanced away.

Well, now. D.J. hoped they hadn't discussed him. If they had, what had Liza said?

"D.J.?" she asked, and he knew he'd missed something. "Do you want a beer, like last night, or a glass of wine?"

"What are you having?"

"Wine."

"Me, too, then. Where can I find a corkscrew?"

"To the left of the sink, top drawer."

After D.J. filled both glasses, he raised his. "To tonight."

Liza copied his gesture. "Tonight," she echoed, the tone of her voice promising an unforgettable evening.

His body began to thrum and a certain part of him

stirred. But now was no time for that. He took a big drink. "Sure there's nothing I can do to help?"

"The salmon is on the grill and should be ready soon, but you can help me carry the rest of the food to the table. How was your day?" she asked as they set out enough food for six people.

"Interesting. Joe came up with an idea for holding on to Island Air."

They moved into the living room, and D.J. shared what he knew.

"I don't know anything about businesses or partnerships," Liza said. "But that sounds promising. How wonderful."

Her smile was so bright, it lit up the room. Along with D.J.'s hopes that the plan might work. "We'll see what my accountant says. He'll probably want to bring in an attorney, and of course Ryan Chase at the bank."

"I'll keep my fingers crossed."

"Keep your fingers crossed?" Liza's grandma repeated, walking into the room. "Hello, D.J., and welcome back."

"Hi, Mrs. H. We're talking about Island Air and the possibility that maybe I won't have to sell. That's a pretty dress. You look good in blue."

"I do?" She blushed. "Thank you, and best of luck with the business. I hate to rush things, but there isn't much time until I leave for my bridge game."

"The salmon is probably cooked," Liza said. "I'll go get it. Everything else is already on the table."

Her grandmother nodded. "Well, then, D.J., let's you and I sit down."

Liza returned with the salmon, and then they passed around the various dishes. The food was excellent, and D.J.

ate with gusto. Before he knew it, they were digging into warm strawberry pie, topped with the ice cream he'd brought along.

"Your appetite is impressive," Liza's grandmother said. "Reminds my of my late husband. I used to love cooking for him, because he always appreciated it so."

"If the food tasted like this, I can see why." D.J. smacked his lips. "That was delicious."

She beamed. "Thank you. Liza deserves some of the credit. She cooked the salmon and made the potato salad." A glance at her watch, and she laid her napkin on the table. "Gracious, look at the time. I'd best go or I'll be late. Sorry to leave you two with the dishes."

D.J. scooted back his chair. "Thank you both for a real treat."

Liza smiled. "It was our pleasure."

Pleasure. The word rang in the air. Every cell in D.J.'s body began to hum. Glad for the table hiding his lap, he swallowed.

"Come back anytime," Mrs. H. said:

"I appreciate the offer." But other than returning to help her move in a few weeks, D.J. doubted he'd be back. After tonight, he and Liza would go their separate ways, free of each other at last. It was what they both wanted.

They all stood up.

"Want me to drive you over, Gram?" Liza asked.

"It's only four miles, and I'm not an invalid. I'll drive myself."

"All right. Have fun." Liza kissed her grandmother's cheek.

The older woman linked her arm through D.J.'s. "Walk me out, D.J."

She moved slowly, and he shortened his steps to match her stride.

At the car, she smiled up at him. "I hope things work out with Island Air and you don't have to sell."

"You and me both." He opened the driver's door for her.

"Liza's a very special woman," she said after buckling her seat belt. "Don't you agree?"

"Uh, yes." D.J. looked into those wise green eyes and knew she'd figured out that something was going on.

Damn. Liza *was* special. She deserved a man who wouldn't break her heart, a man willing to commit. And he wasn't that guy. For that reason, he couldn't make love with her tonight—even if he wanted her more than he'd ever wanted any woman.

"Drive safe, now," he said. "And thanks again for dinner."

"You're welcome." Mrs. Haverford gave a satisfied nod. She started the car and backed slowly into the turnaround, missing the Harley by scant inches. When she pulled onto the street, D.J. trudged inside. Liza was in the kitchen, washing pots and pans. He cleared the plates from the dining room and brought them to the sink.

"Ready for seconds on pie?" She tossed her head flirtatiously, something D.J. had never seen her do. "Or would you rather try a different kind of dessert?"

Man, did he want that. Turning her down was the toughest thing he'd ever done. He shook his head. "I can't stay."

In the process of drying her hands on a dish towel, Liza widened her eyes. "What?"

"Making love with you. Well, it isn't such a smart idea."

Her eyes narrowed. "Exactly what did my grandmother say to you out there?"

"Nothing, I swear. It's just, if you got hurt… I don't want that on my conscience."

Now she looked exasperated. "I'm not some naive young girl, D.J. I'm a grown woman with real needs. You've been honest with me, and I've been honest with you. Yes, I'd like to get married and start a family. I have a plan for that. When I have a new job and I've moved, I'm going to focus on finding a man who wants those things, too. But that could be a month or six weeks from now— or who knows when? I haven't had sex in three years, and if you don't make love with me tonight, I swear, I'll die of frustration."

D.J. understood completely. He was about there himself.

"I had myself tested after Timothy left," she continued, "and I'm healthy. How about you?"

"I am."

"Good. We have two and a half hours until Gram comes back. Need I say more?"

Her pleading eyes searched his face, and there was no way he could resist. He lifted the corner of his mouth. "You should've been a lawyer, you make such a good argument. All right, but not here." Not in her grandmother's house. "My place isn't much, but I do have a big bed. And it's clean—I changed the sheets yesterday. Best leave your grandma a note so she won't worry, since you're going to be out late."

Liza scribbled something on a piece of paper and left it on the counter. Then she took his hand and pulled him toward the door.

Without speaking, they donned helmets and climbed onto the Harley. Ten minutes later, D.J. pulled in to a parking space in front of his building.

LIZA BARELY HAD TIME to take in D.J.'s studio apartment before his mouth claimed hers. His arms around her felt like heaven—just where Liza wanted to be. Yet as badly as·she'd yearned for this, she was still a little scared. D.J. was right—and if she wasn't careful she might get hurt. She would keep her heart safe, she promised herself. What happened tonight was physical, nothing more.

D.J. deepened the kiss, his mouth hot and demanding. No man had ever kissed her with such passion. Liza forgot about everything else.

Her body throbbed for more, and suddenly she was damp between her legs. Her fierce desire seemed to melt her bones. Unable to stand and desperate for more, she clung to him and broke the kiss. "I need to get out of these clothes."

Standing before the drawn window shade, she stepped out of her sandals and then drew her shirt over her head. Slowly, she unhooked her bra and removed it, and was rewarded by D.J.'s heated expression.

Keeping his gaze on her, he removed his shirt. His upper arms and chest were solid and muscled without being overly so. His belly was lean and flat. Below that, she could see his arousal.

"See what you do to me." His eyes glittered with need.

Feeling sexy and desirable, and acting purely on instinct, Liza cupped her breasts.

Never had D.J. seen a more seductive woman. He let out a groan. "You are amazing."

"You make me feel sexy."

She licked her lips and the thought of that mouth on him drove him wild. He reached for her and pulled her close.

The feel of her breasts against his chest was pure torture. Plundering her mouth with the steamiest kisses of his life, he moved her toward the bed on unsteady legs.

He lay down, on his back, with Liza resting against him. She flicked her tongue across his nipples. And again. Blood roared through his head. He hadn't been this turned on since… He'd *never* been this turned on.

Changing positions so that he was on top, he took her mouth once more. Dropped to the sensitive place below her ear, then moved down the smooth column of her neck, across her delicate collarbone, to her swollen breasts. Her taut nipples tasted as sweet as he remembered.

She moaned and urged him nearer. "I've been dreaming about this."

"Me, too, all the time. You are so sweet."

He teased and sucked until she was writhing under him, her pleasure fueling his desire all the more. *His.*

"I need you," she whispered, unbuttoning her jeans.

What those words did to him. He helped her slide off her jeans and panties, then stopped to look at her. She was slender and fair-skinned. Her neck and her breasts were flushed with desire and her lips were pink and slightly swollen.

Aroused and eager. For him.

"I love your legs, your breasts," he growled. "You're perfect."

"Thank you." Tears filled her eyes.

Uh-oh. In the process of sliding his palm down her smooth belly, he stilled. "Having second thoughts?"

"No! It's just… It's been a while since anyone's told me I was beautiful."

"Any man who doesn't think so is blind." He slid his hand below her navel to the apex of her thighs.

Her legs parted. Heart hammering in his chest, he stroked the soft skin of her inner thigh and slowly moved toward the most sensitive part of her. As he inched nearer, she tensed and ever so slightly raised her hips. It was all he could do not to strip down and take her right then. But this first time was about her. He fingered her tiny, moist nub. A small, breathy sound issued from her throat, and she pushed up, against his hand. Still teasing this most sensitive place, D.J. slipped two fingers inside. She was so wet and slick, he almost went over the edge himself.

Soon, he thought. But not just yet. He knelt between her legs. Parting her folds, he licked her swollen sweetness, all the while moving his fingers inside her. Every time he sensed she was near to climaxing he eased off, taking his sweet time until he was half-crazed with her woman scent—and she was frantic with desire.

Suddenly, she let out a deep, throaty sound, clutched his shoulders and convulsed around his fingers.

When she finally relaxed, D.J. kissed her inner thighs and raised his head. Her mouth was curled into a contented smile. She looked satisfied and thoroughly loved.

The most beautiful woman he'd ever known.

"Did you enjoy that?" he asked, moving up to lie beside her.

"It was wonderful." She kissed him, a long, deep kiss. "I can taste myself on you, and it's turning me on all over again."

D.J.'s groin twitched and he moaned. "That's about the sexiest thing I've ever heard."

"I can see that." She glanced down at him and smiled, a woman aware of her feminine power. "Take off your pants."

"I aim to please." In record time D.J. had kicked off his jeans and boxers.

She stared admiringly at his arousal, then cupped him and slid her hand slowly up and down his shaft. His body coiled tight, and he knew he was close to losing control. He caught hold of her wrist and lifted her hand. "I'm about to embarrass myself. Just a sec."

Turning away, he took a foil packet from the pocket of his jeans, opened it and sheathed himself. "Now, where were we?" He covered her with his body, his arousal pressing against her.

"Right there," she whispered, levering her hips.

Sweet Lord. Not plunging into her was torture. Arms trembling, he held himself poised above her. "I'm going to make this so good for you, Liza."

Her eyes were wide and certain. "It's already pretty darned good."

She hooked her legs around his hips and arched toward him. Closing his eyes, he sank into her as far as he could. *Home.*

For one brief moment he held still, savoring the feel of the moist heat that enfolded him like a glove. Until she squeezed her inner muscles.

His tenuous control snapped. "I. Can't. Hold. Back." He spoke—barely—through gritted teeth.

"I don't want you to. Hurry."

He did just that, in and out, faster and deeper, until there was nothing but him and Liza and the exquisite buildup of tension.

Sounds he already recognized rippled out from deep in her throat. She clenched herself around him, her release beginning. As her own climax deepened, his unfolded. Everything faded into the most intense pleasure of his life.

When it was over and the world righted itself again, he kissed her once more and rolled onto his back, so that she was resting on his chest. "That was amazing."

"I was thinking, fantastic." She tipped up her head to smile lazily at him. "Better than I ever imagined."

"That makes two of us. I'll be right back." He slipped into the bathroom to clean up, then brought a warm, damp cloth back to bed and gently did the same for her.

"Thank you," she said. "You're such a thoughtful man."

No lover had ever said that to him. As spent as he was, he wanted her again. And maybe another time after that. Good thing there was a full box of condoms in the drawer.

"You think this is thoughtful?" Smiling, he tossed the cloth onto the floor, then reached for her. "Baby, I'm just getting started."

HOURS LATER, D.J. awoke. Liza lay curled beside him. They'd dozed and made love twice more. Each time his need for her grew stronger. Now near dawn, he wanted her a fourth time.

He knew he'd want her again after that, too. A lifetime of Liza's loving....

Whoa. Where had *that* come from? Scared, he sat bolt upright. There was no light around the edges of the window shade. He squinted at the clock. It was 4:00 a.m. He gently nudged her awake. "I have to go to work soon."

"Okay." Looking sleepy and seductive, her hair tangled

from their night of passion, Liza stretched and propped herself up. "And I should get home before Gram is awake."

"Do you want to shower first?" he offered.

To his relief, she shook her head. "I'll do that at home."

He'd drop her off, then come back here.

For the ride home she borrowed his jean jacket. As she got off the bike in her grandmother's driveway, he knew he should ask about getting together again, but his feelings had him too damn terrified.

Slipping out of the jacket, Liza frowned. "D.J.? Is something wrong?"

"Everything's great." He forced a grin and tucked the jacket into the leather pouch. Caught a whiff of her scent and winced.

Knowing she expected a kiss, he briefly touched her lips. "See you, Liza."

Chapter Twelve

The house was silent, meaning Gram was still asleep. Thank goodness. Liza had no intention of answering any prying questions. Tired and confused, she crept upstairs to shower.

She'd just enjoyed the best lovemaking of her life. But at some point her need for D.J. had become more than physical. It had moved to her heart. She was in love with him, a secret never to be shared with anyone. Especially not D.J.

Though her heart ached as she washed off his masculine scent and the smells of their lovemaking, she marveled at the satisfied, contented feeling in her body. D.J. was a thorough and generous lover, and she was certain he'd enjoyed the lovemaking as much as she had.

Yet when he'd dropped her off he couldn't even meet her eyes, couldn't leave fast enough.

For the life of her, Liza didn't understand why. She was positive that D.J. had no idea about her true feelings for him, so it wasn't that. Possibly he was the bed 'em, then leave 'em type—a man who wanted nothing to do with a woman after sex. But, no, D.J. wasn't like that. Was he? She never had been the best judge of men.

Mentally smacking her forehead—how could she have been so foolish?—she toweled dry, then put on her pajamas. But she was too keyed up to sleep. Donning a robe, she headed downstairs to make coffee, thoughts whirling through her mind.

D.J. had tried to talk her out of making love. *She'd* been the one to coax *him*. A bed 'em, then leave 'em kind of man wouldn't have done that. They'd agreed that after this one night, they'd be finished with each other. In light of that, D.J.'s behavior almost made sense.

Unless one of them fell in love with the other.

Had she truly believed that after one night with the man she'd be able to get over her need for him? Not really. A fine mess she was in. Releasing a heavy sigh, she measured out the coffee and filled the coffeemaker with water.

How in the world did she expect to fall in love with a marriage-minded man, when she already was in love with D.J.? When the coffee was ready she took a mug to the table, sat down and leafed through a magazine, since the next *Halo Island Weekly* wouldn't be out until Monday. She thumbed through, looking for something interesting to read. Five minutes later she gave up. It was no use. Her mind was too full of what had just happened and what it meant for her. She couldn't concentrate.

The house was way too quiet, so she opened a window. Instantly, the soft sound of the waves warmed the silence. The clock over the stove said it was almost six. Gram would be up soon.

Liza wondered what she'd say to her grandmother.

Half an hour later, Gram scuffed into the kitchen in her robe and terry-cloth slippers. When she saw Liza sitting there, she looked surprised.

"Goodness, you're up early. You were out so late, I was sure you'd sleep in. Did you and D.J. have fun last night?"

Liza nodded. She had no intention of elaborating. But Gram's loving interest changed her mind.

"You were right about me, Gram. All along I've had feelings for D.J. And after last night I realized I've fallen in love with him."

"Oh, honey. That's wonderful. I was hoping you two—"

Liza held up her hand, silencing her grandmother. "This isn't good news. I can't tell him how I feel, because he doesn't want my love."

Her grandmother looked stricken. "I'm so sorry. What can I do to help?"

"There's nothing either of us can do," Liza said. "But everything will be all right. I'm strong—and eventually I'll get over him."

Stating it aloud, she knew that she would.

MONDAY AFTERNOON, having hired a sub to take his flights for him yet again, D.J. sat facing Carter Boyle across his expansive desk. Located in downtown Halo Island, Carter's office was twice the size of D.J.'s and ten times as plush, a testament to the CPA's success. His reputation was excellent and his business continued to grow.

D.J. wanted that kind of success and was sure he'd get it, someday. At the moment, however, simply holding on to Island Air was enough.

He'd just told his accountant about the partnership that

Joe and the others had proposed. "What do you think?" he asked, watching Carter closely.

Eyes slightly narrowed, the CPA hesitated. "I like it."

"I sense a 'but.'"

"I know how you feel about partnerships. You don't trust them. Heck, you decided to put the business you love on the market rather than find a partner." Carter steepled his hands and tapped his fingers against his chin. "I don't understand why you're thinking of changing your mind."

This was the reason D.J. had scheduled this appointment. Carter wasn't afraid to speak his mind and ask tough questions. D.J. *had* changed, in a big way, and having thought about this exact question over the past few days, he was ready with the answer.

"Like you said, it's a trust issue. These employees have been with me since day one. I trust them and they trust me. They're loyal, too. If I hold the majority share in the company, I'll still be the decision maker. They tell me that's the way they want it, with me setting policy and making decisions and them enjoying our future profits. Call me a fool, but I believe them."

"Those are sound reasons," Carter said. "With a solid legal agreement to back it all up, I think this thing could work."

D.J. let out the breath he'd been holding. "That's good news. I guess I should talk with Mason Green, huh?" The attorney who had drawn up—and later dissolved—D.J.'s partnership with Ethan.

Carter nodded. "He'll iron out the details and prepare the papers. But first, talk to Ryan Chase and get his okay. Without that, the rest is pointless."

Leaning back in his leather chair, D.J. mulled everything

over. "He's never visited Island Air. I'll invite him to take a tour and meet the people who want to be my partners."

Once Chase saw how tight and interested the group was, he'd be all for this partnership. D.J. hoped. He thought about what Liza would say when he told her, and how her face would brighten. Only he wasn't going to see or talk to her.

"Keep me in the loop," Carter said.

"Will do. Do you want to be there for the tour?"

"You don't need me. Now that you have a game plan, try to get some sleep. You look like you could use it."

Carter didn't know the half of it. D.J. hadn't slept well in weeks, but the past few nights had been even worse. It'd been four days since that mind-blowing night with Liza and he'd been too mixed up for a decent night's rest, scared that he cared too much.

He now realized that what he felt for Liza was lust, plain and simple. He liked her, too. A lot. But the things she wanted—love and marriage and kids? D.J. wasn't ready for any of that. His main focus was the airline. And anyway, Liza would probably be offered that job in Seattle. She didn't do long-distance relationships. And neither did D.J. He didn't do relationships, period.

It was a good thing he'd figured it all out.

"It's been a rough few weeks," he said. "When the dust settles, maybe we'll share a pitcher."

"Sounds good."

"I'll be in touch."

He walked down the hallway, the sound of his footsteps muffled by the thick carpet. His thoughts were on the woman who had caused such havoc in his already stress-ful life. For the first time since his marriage had gone sour he trusted a woman. He'd never expected that. Liza was great to talk to, fun to tease and the best bed partner he'd ever known.

But as badly as he wanted to get her naked again—and he thought about that constantly—he wasn't about to pursue the idea. Wasn't about to see her, period.

For that reason he hadn't called her, and was staying away from places where he might run into her. Which, on Halo Island, was just about everywhere. Aside from brief trips to grab lunch or dinner, he hung around the office or took the Harley for a solitary spin. No stopping at the park or visiting any bars. Better for both of them this way.

He missed her, though. But avoiding Liza at all costs was necessary. Never mind why. He wasn't about to go there.

Coward, a voice in his head scolded. "I'm no coward," he muttered. Then snickered. Now he was talking to himself. That just went to show how crazy this whole Liza business was.

TUESDAY AFTERNOON, Liza's grandmother sank wearily against the living-room sofa cushions. "I'm glad that's over and done with."

Liza glanced at the six-shelf glass curio cabinet built into the corner, which the two of them had just cleaned out. Over the years Gram and Grandpop had collected many figurines and models, some of them quite valuable, to commemorate birthdays, anniversaries and other special events. There were enough to fill the cabinet and then some.

Although Diane, Uncle Jake, Mark, Charlene and Paul had taken the few pieces they wanted, there'd still been dozens left to sort through. A job that should have taken a few hours at most, but instead had consumed most of the day. Mainly because each piece came with memories and stories, and Gram had shared them all.

Liza had listened carefully, even taking notes so she'd remember the details that chronicled her grandparents' lives.

"I hope I didn't bore you too much," Gram said.

"Are you kidding? I love hearing about you and Grandpop."

They'd shared a deep and abiding love, and Liza yearned for what they'd had. She intended to find it, too. Once she was over D.J.

Gram smiled. "It was fun to relive some of the wonderful times Harold and I shared. Even though he's been gone nearly twenty years, I still miss him."

"I do, too, Gram."

Both were silent, each wrapped in her own thoughts.

Naturally, everything in Liza's mind related to D.J. In the five days since their night of lovemaking, the man hadn't so much as telephoned. Which was rude, but not unexpected.

After all, she'd assured D.J. that she wanted only that one evening together. He was supposed to be out of her system and vice versa. Apparently, the plan had worked for him. Liza wasn't so lucky.

"You could call him," Gram said, as if she'd read Liza's mind. "And invite him to watch the fireworks with us." Fourth of July was this Friday.

"Call who?" Liza asked, feigning ignorance. But her grandmother knew her too well. At her don't-try-to-fool-me look, Liza gave that up. "I'm not about to chase after D.J. Hatcher. If he's interested, he can invite *me* to watch the fireworks with *him*."

Her grandmother chuckled. "That's the way I always played the game."

"There is no game."

"Of course there is—chase, play hard to get and allow yourself to be caught. Whenever you put males and females together, they do one of the three. The game continues until they fall in love and get married. Sometimes, it goes on even after the wedding. At least it did with Harold and me, whenever we argued."

"You two never argued."

"We certainly did. Now and then, every couple does. I know you, and after that dinner with D.J. I feel that I know him a little, too. You are definitely playing the game. At the moment you've simply stumbled a bit, that's all."

"It's more than a stumble."

"Isn't there something you can do, some way of fixing that?" Gram asked.

"That's up to D.J. Have you heard the phone ring? Neither have I." Liza hugged her waist. "He's no longer interested, Gram."

Her grandmother gave her a thoughtful look. "I hate to see you so downhearted, right when you were starting to get your confidence back."

Liza was beginning to wish she'd never shared her feelings about D.J. At least Gram hadn't said a word to Diane, who was leaving with Art tomorrow afternoon, heading for Seattle via seaplane, then spending the night near SeaTac Airport for the following morning's flight to Australia. Liza dearly hoped D.J. wasn't their pilot on the flight from Halo Island.

"At least I know for certain that I'm capable of falling in love again," she said. "After Timothy, I wasn't so sure."

Gram opened her mouth. Unable to bear another word about D.J. and love, Liza changed the subject. "Boy, am I hungry, and dinner isn't for hours yet. How about an iced tea and one of those peaches I bought at the market?"

"All right, then, change the subject. Tea and a peach would be lovely."

As Liza headed for the kitchen, her cell phone rang. Could it be D.J.? Darned if her heart didn't begin to beat a little faster. She slid the phone from her purse. A glance at the LED told her it was the Seattle school district.

Stifling a pang of disappointment, she chided herself for even hoping it might be D.J.—this call was a positive thing, wasn't it? They must want to interview her.

"Hello?" she said.

When she brought out the teapot a few minutes later, she delivered her good news. "That was the Seattle school district, asking me to interview on Monday morning."

Her grandmother tried to smile. "Of course I'm happy for you, because I know you want a teaching job. But I'm also selfish. I want you to set down roots on Halo Island, in this house. That way we can see each other all the time."

"You know I'd like that, too, Gram."

But even if there were teaching jobs, Liza didn't know how she could stand to live here. Especially if things worked out at Island Air and D.J. stayed on the island. She'd always be looking around, wondering if she'd run into him, and she'd never be able to relax. What fun was that?

Until she was far away from D.J., she'd never get over him. A job in Seattle was exactly what she needed.

"Are you going to call your mother and let her know about the interview?" Gram asked.

"I'll tell her and Art when I drive them to Island Air tomorrow." Liza intended to drop them off and leave, just in case D.J. happened to be in the lobby. "I think I'll catch the early-morning ferry to Anacortes Monday, and then drive to Seattle." Which meant a forty-five-minute ferry ride followed by a ninety-minute drive. "May I borrow your car?"

"That's a long trip, Liza, especially with the tourist traffic. It'll take you all day just to get there and back, and my car doesn't get the best mileage. Wouldn't you rather fly?"

A sly gleam flashed in Gram's eyes, and Liza knew what she was thinking—that if she and D.J. saw each other on the flight, they might get together. Liza didn't want that. She didn't want to see him at all. "The ferry is cheaper and more relaxing," she said. "I'll bring a book to read while I'm waiting."

"All right, if that's what you want to do."

As D.J. READIED THE PLANE for his only flight Wednesday afternoon, he whistled happily. After a tour and an early-morning meeting with Ryan Chase and D.J.'s future partners, Chase had given what he called a provisional okay to the partnership. He thought that the employees investing in the company sounded good, but he needed to look at their finances and tax returns. Joe had agreed to collect the papers and deliver them to the bank on Monday. That same day, D.J. was meeting with his attorney.

Thirty minutes before flight time, passengers sauntered down the floating dock toward him. Damned if Liza's mother and the man who must be her stepfather weren't at the front of the group. Of all the people… D.J. had no idea what Liza had told them about the other night. He still hadn't called her, and as wise a decision as that was, his conscience bothered him.

They were only ten feet away now, with Diane hurrying toward him. The only thing to do was make nice. D.J. smiled. "Hello."

"I was hoping you'd be piloting this plane," Liza's mother said. "I asked Liza and she didn't know. This is my husband, Art."

D.J. shook the man's hand. They were nearly the same height, and Art's grip was firm.

"Heard a lot about you," Art said.

"Yeah?" D.J. wondered what Liza had said. "You're a retired stockbroker, right? Looks as if you're both fully recovered from the other night. Where are you two headed?"

"Liza didn't tell you? We're going to Australia for a month, to celebrate our first wedding anniversary. Which happens to be today."

"Uh, we haven't talked lately. Happy anniversary."

"Thank you," Diane said. "I thought you and Liza were friends. Well, that explains it."

"Explains what?"

"Why she hasn't mentioned you. But then, she never tells me anything. Her own mother!" Diane sniffed. "You probably don't know that she has a job interview on Monday. In Seattle."

"Good for her."

D.J. told himself he was glad for Liza, that she was out of his system and he was out of hers. Yeah, right, and there was a million dollars in his bank account.

"But not for her grandmother or me. We want her to

stay on the island. What a shame there's no one special to keep her here."

She gave him a meaningful look, and D.J. figured she meant him. Which was not happening. He nodded at a family of four and helped them board. When he finished, Art was waiting.

"Heard you're selling the company," he said in a low voice. "Have you had any offers?"

Both he and Diane leaned in, as if they expected to hear something for their ears only.

"No," said D.J. "But that's okay. I've decided to take the business off the market."

"Oh?" Diane tilted her head, her sharp eyes probing.

He saw no reason to hide what he was doing, since everyone at Island Air knew. "I'm working on a deal that will allow the employees to invest in the company. They'll be given shares depending on how much they put in."

"A limited partnership." Looking impressed, Art stroked his chin. "Not a bad idea."

"Does Liza know about this?" Diane asked.

D.J. nodded.

To his surprise, her mom looked hurt. "See there, Art? She doesn't tell me anything."

Art patted her shoulder and exchanged a what's-a-man-supposed-to-do look with D.J. "Let it go, princess. This is our anniversary. Why don't we board now, and take our seats."

"All right, but when we get to Seattle I'm calling her."

D.J. figured he should alert Liza. Anybody would, he told himself. He wanted to know more about the interview, too.

At the thought of talking to her, he felt way too happy.

He didn't like that one bit. He wouldn't call, he decided.
Yet a few minutes before boarding, he pulled out his cell
phone and punched in her number.

Chapter Thirteen

Liza was cleaning up the lunch dishes while Gram napped, when the kitchen phone rang. Not wanting the sound to wake her grandmother, she snatched up the receiver. "Hello?"

"Hey, there. It's D.J."

As if she didn't recognize that deep, sexy voice. Her heart seemed to stop. "Hi." Stretching out the cord, she sank onto the banquette.

"Uh, how are you?"

It'd been almost a week since their night together. What had taken him so long? "Terrific," she said, hoping she sounded convincing. Over the phone she heard the squawk of seagulls. "Where are you?"

"About to take off for Seattle. Your mom and Art are on the flight."

Liza groaned. "You didn't say anything, did you?" Not that there was anything to say. What had happened with her and D.J. was over and done with.

"About us? No, and judging by the conversation we had, I guess you didn't, either."

"The subject hasn't come up." Liza liked how that sounded, as if there were nothing at all between her and D.J.

"They asked about Island Air. When I told them what was happening, your mom kind of got upset that you hadn't told her. Said she was calling you from Seattle."

"Great," Liza muttered. "Thanks for the warning."

"Sure thing."

Silence hung in the air. The man had waited six days to call, and she refused to be anything but distant and polite. Or to keep this conversation going. She tapped her fingers on the tabletop.

"She told me about your job interview in Seattle."

"Bright and early Monday morning."

"That'll be on my flight."

"Gram's loaning me her car. I decided to take the ferry and drive."

"Flying is faster."

Liza said nothing.

After a lengthy pause, D.J. cleared his throat. "How's your grandma's packing going?"

"Slowly. It's draining." *Do you think about that incredible night together as often as I do?*

"I can imagine."

"Who are you talking to, Liza?" Gram called out.

Apparently, she'd finished her nap.

"It's D.J.," Liza answered without covering the mouthpiece.

Her grandmother wandered into the kitchen. "What does he want?"

"Gram wants to know why you called."

"Couple of reasons. Your grandma moves next week-end. What time should I come over?"

Liza half wished he hadn't offered to help. Seeing him and pretending she didn't care wouldn't be easy. But they needed his help. "How about nine?"

"Okay. Hey, I gave Ryan Chase a tour of Island Air this morning. He was impressed with both the company and the employees. The next steps are for him to look over every-one's financial records and for my lawyer to set up the part-nership. If things go the way I think they will, I'll take the company off the market. Something I shared with your mom and stepdad."

With news that exciting, Liza forgot about keeping a cool distance. "Oh, D.J., that's wonderful."

"Thanks," he said, and she heard the warmth in his voice.

"Invite him to watch the fireworks with us," Gram whis-pered.

Was she out of her mind? Frowning, Liza made a stern face and shook her head. "I have things to do, D.J., and I really should go. Thanks again for the warning."

"And I have a plane to fly. Bye, Liza."

PLANNING TO AVOID the crowd and skip this year's fire-works, D.J. joined Joe and some other friends for a barbecue in the park. For several hours they tossed Frisbees, stuffed themselves on burgers, chicken and a half-dozen side dishes, and shared a lot of laughs. But as relaxing and enjoyable as the afternoon was, he was restless. Eventually, he left and by dusk he was striding across the beach, not far from where he'd first kissed Liza.

He'd thought a lot about their chilly conversation two

days ago. She was mad at him, and he needed to talk to her in person. At some place that was safe, where he wouldn't do what he wanted to and start up with her again.

With the hordes of men, women and children in portable chairs or on blankets, waiting for the fireworks to start, this was just the right sort of place.

He knew she'd be here, but where? he wondered, scanning the crowd.

At last he spotted her, seated on a lawn chair beside her grandma. She was laughing, her head back and her expression carefree. D.J.'s heart felt as if it were about to burst from his chest. Damn, but it was good to see her. Too good. She didn't notice him, and if he were smart he'd turn around and leave before she did. Yet he started toward her, weaving between frolicking kids and adults.

He knew exactly when she noticed him. Her eyes widened, then narrowed, and her pretty smile faded. She did not look pleased.

Her grandma smiled, though. "Hello, D.J. How nice to see you."

"You, too, Mrs. H. Happy Fourth."

"Same to you."

D.J. planted his feet in front of Liza. "Can I talk to you?" Her grandma looked way too interested, so he added, "Privately?"

"All right." He offered Liza a hand up, but she ignored him. "I'll be right back, Gram."

Of course, there was no place private to go. D.J. forgot that he'd wanted a crowd, for safety purposes. In fact, what he wanted was to be alone. To kiss and touch Liza and melt her coolness. He settled for a walk.

"It's great to see you," he said, ambling beside her.

She gave him a disbelieving look. "Let's be honest here, D.J. If you really wanted to see me, you'd have stopped by Gram's or asked me out. Or called once in a while."

Even angry, she was cute. D.J. guessed that every little boy she'd ever taught had had a major crush on her.

"I did call, the other day," he said. "And in case you forgot, I'm working day and night, flying and doing my best to save my company."

"The same things you've been doing since I got here. Yet you found time to take me to that private rock for lunch and to come over to Gram's for dinner two nights in a row. And to spend most of a night with me."

The look she gave him, one eyebrow slightly raised, made him feel rotten.

"I thought we weren't going to get involved," he said, but even to his own ears it sounded like a lame excuse.

"That doesn't mean we ignore each other, as if we're sorry for what happened. I'm not sorry, and I don't want to be ignored. It's jerky, D.J."

Guilty as charged. He'd been avoiding her and they both knew it. Well, crap. He rubbed the back of his neck. "You're right. I guess I was playing it safe."

Lips compressed, arms crossed, Liza continued to eye him.

Now, why had he said that? Not about to explain what he didn't understand himself, he ducked his head. "Okay, I should have called. Sorry."

For a few more seconds her lips stayed tight and thin. Then she uncrossed her arms and relaxed. "You're forgiven."

"So everything's okay with us? We're still friends?"

"I suppose."

That was good enough for him. He blew out a relieved breath.

"Casual, platonic friends," she added. "No kissing or touching. We're done with that."

"Right," he said, while wanting her more than ever. "Are you nervous about Monday?"

"You mean the interview? Of course I am. Those things always put me on edge."

"I'm sure you'll do fine."

"I hope so. I really need this job."

D.J. knew that. He knew it was best that she got what she wanted. But if she did, he'd only see her when she visited the island. Maybe not even then. This seriously bothered him—he didn't want to care as much as he did.

"Anything new with Island Air?" Liza asked.

"There's a meeting Monday night after we close, with the lawyer and my soon-to-be partners. It'll take a while to iron out the details, but by the end of the month the whole thing will be settled."

"That's great. You must be so pleased."

He waited for her to smile and be happy for him. She did smile, but not the amazing light-up-your-face way she had before.

"It's getting dark," she said. "I should get back to my grandmother."

"I'll walk you over."

"No, thanks. Enjoy the fireworks."

She didn't invite him to sit with her and he didn't ask. It was best this way. What mattered was that they were friends again. Exactly what D.J. wanted.

Yet as he watched her walk away, he thought of ways to make her want him again and look at him as if he was important to her. Thoroughly confused, he frowned.

Before the fireworks started, he was on his bike—heading away from Liza and the beach.

As THE FERRY pulled away from the Anacortes harbor and headed for Halo Island on Monday afternoon, Liza stayed in the car. She would call and let Gram know she was on the way back. She turned on her cell phone, which had been off since before her interview this morning. To her surprise there was a message from Tina. She listened to it before calling her grandmother.

"Guess what I just heard?" Tina said. "There's an opening at school this fall. The fourth-grade teacher is taking a semester off to care for her sick father. It's not a permanent position, but it would give the teachers and principal a chance to get to know you. I hope you don't mind, but I told Marsha Devaney about you. Remember her—the school administrator? She said to call her. Let me know what happens, okay? It's been a while, so call me anyway, and tell me about things.

"Oh, there's also a bunco game tonight at the community center. I always have such a good time. Want to go?"

If by "things" she meant D.J., Liza had nothing to say. Since seeing him on the beach on the Fourth of July, she'd thought of him often. And of their conversation.

Liza was proud of herself for saying she wanted to be casual, platonic friends. But pretending she didn't love him when she did seemed beyond difficult. She couldn't be his friend, and after Gram's move next weekend she wasn't likely to see him again.

As for that one-semester job on the island, Liza needed full-time work—anyplace but Halo Island. Gram could always come visit her. After the positive interview today, Liza had a strong feeling she'd be moving to Seattle. Where she would absolutely, positively get over D.J. and find a man who wanted and deserved her love.

She called her grandmother. "I'm on the ferry back, about half an hour from the island."

"Then you'll be home way before dinner. Good. How was the interview?"

"It went really well. I'm pretty sure they'll offer me the job. The principal said she'd let me know by Thursday. I'll tell you more when I get back. Before I hang up, is it okay if I play bunco with Tina tonight?"

"I've heard about that—something the community center has started. Go, and have fun. You must've gotten her message. She called the house earlier, after trying your cell phone. I told her about the interview. She didn't know about that, but she *did* know about an opening at Halo Island School. Did you know about that fourth-grade teacher who will be gone for a semester?"

"I just listened to her message, so, yes. See you soon."

Liza hung up and phoned Tina to make plans.

Back at Gram's house later, they sipped iced tea in the breakfast nook. Gram was moving on Saturday, and in the morning they'd start packing the kitchen items she would take with her.

"Tell me about the interview," Gram said.

"It's a third-grade class in a nice school, and a continuing contract. Just what I want."

"Wonderful. But just in case, maybe you should apply for the semester job here on the island."

"But that only lasts half a year. What would I do then?"

"What you've done before. Substitute teach."

"Here on the island? With one small school, I can't imagine I'd be working much. You yourself said that I should put down roots. If I get this continuing contract in Seattle, I'll finally be able to do that. Seattle isn't so far away—it's a heck of a lot shorter commute than Bellingham. You can visit anytime." And if she needed to—if her grandmother took sick or something—she could get back fast.

Liza prayed that would never happen. But if it did, she hoped someone she didn't know would be piloting the plane. Anyone but D.J. Hatcher.

"You already have roots right here," Gram said. "You never know, the semester job could turn into something permanent. And you'd be living in this house, a house you say you love, with no monthly payments to worry about. You wouldn't have to see that much of your mother, either. You've seen how busy she and Art are."

Everything Gram said was true. But how could Liza possibly stay here? Loving a man who didn't love her was painful and she wanted to move on. Accepting a permanent position in a good school district seemed the perfect way to do that.

"If I do get the job, I'll need to find an apartment in Seattle. And it'll take a while to pack up the one in Bellingham. Bill and Noreen, the friends who are staying in my apartment, are about to move into their new house, so the timing works out."

"You're telling me you won't be staying as long as you planned."

"I'll probably leave as soon as you're moved in and I've had a chance to clean up around here."

"I see," Gram said. "This leaving-early business has to do with D.J., doesn't it? When he didn't sit with us for the fireworks, I knew you two still weren't getting along."

"I couldn't invite him, Gram. He wants to be friends, but I can't." Liza glanced at her sweating iced-tea glass, then bit her lip.

Her grandmother gave her a sage look. "I think he wants more than that. He just isn't able to verbalize his feelings. Some men can't."

Oh, D.J. had shared his feelings, all right. He didn't want to get involved. "I don't think so, Gram. There are lots of other single guys out there, and one of them will be the right man for me. Seattle's a big city, and I just know I'll find my future husband there."

"I can't fault your attitude." Gram smiled, then sipped her drink. "But tell me, if D.J. *was* romantically interested in you, would you take the teaching job on the island?"

"Why even think about that? He isn't and he never will be."

"But if he *was?*"

There was no sense trying to fool her grandmother. Liza sighed. "If he wanted to marry me and have kids? I'd stay in a heartbeat."

AFTER A SUCCESSFUL meeting with the attorney and D.J.'s coworkers once Island Air had closed Monday night, he and Joe headed for the parking lot.

"You want to go for a beer?" Joe asked.

D.J. glanced at his watch. It was just after nine and he wanted to stop by Liza's grandma's before it got too late, with boxes for the move. At least, that was his excuse. Truth was, he needed to see Liza. He told himself it was because he had more news to share—tonight's meeting had gone well, and the partnership was practically a done deal—and she had asked to know what was happening.

"Can we take a rain check on that? I've got plans."

"Hot date?"

The only woman D.J. wanted was supposed to be out of his system. He shrugged. "No such luck."

"I feel your pain," Joe said. Brianna was out of town again, and he was pining for her.

Minutes later, D.J. turned the pickup into Mrs. Haverford's driveway, looking forward to seeing Liza way more than was smart. Juggling boxes, he pushed the doorbell. The door opened. Instead of Liza, her grandma stood there.

"Hey there, Mrs. H.," he said, wondering where Liza was.

"Why, D.J., what a lovely surprise."

"Thought you could use these boxes for the move."

"How sweet." Smiling at him with genuine affection, she opened the screen door and gestured him inside. "You can stack them against the wall."

D.J. wiped his feet and stepped inside. "Is Liza around?" he asked after he set down the boxes.

"Unfortunately, no. She and Tina are at the community center, playing bunco. I expect she'll be home quite late."

His disappointment was both sharp and bewildering. Mrs. Haverford's scrutiny only added to his agitation. D.J. pulled on his ear. "She had her interview today. How'd it go?"

"Very well. She's expecting a job offer later in the week."

"That's great," he said.

Only it wasn't. Not for him. Feeling hollow inside, he aligned the boxes. He'd known Liza wouldn't stay on the island, so why did he feel so empty?

Because, lunkhead. She's more than a friend.

He was in love with Liza.

The realization cleared up all the confusion. D.J. straightened. When and how had *that* happened? What did it matter? The point was, he was crazy about her. It had been years since he'd felt like this about a woman.

Too bad she didn't feel the same about him. He recalled her cool attitude on the beach the other night and winced. What did he expect? After making love with her, he'd all but ignored her for days.

Well, hell.

Her grandma was watching him with a shrewd look. D.J. cleared his throat and started for the door. "Will you tell her I stopped by, and that I said congratulations?"

She nodded. "I will."

On the drive home, he thought about winning Liza back. Back? He'd never had her in the first place—not her heart, anyway.

He thought about telling her how he felt, then dismissed the idea as nuts. Lay his heart on the line? Too risky, and his pride wouldn't let him. He'd best stay away from Liza Miller. But he'd promised to help with the move. He considered reneging on the offer, but he couldn't do that to Mrs. Haverford.

There was only one way to make it through moving day—keep it light and paste a smile on his face. Once he moved Mrs. H.'s things into her new place, he was done with both of them.

He would date women, lots of women. Have fun and good times the way he used to.

Pretty soon, he'd forget all about Liza Miller.

Chapter Fourteen

Thursday afternoon, after wrapping most of the good china that Gram wanted to take with her, Liza paused to rub the small of her back. With the move in two days, there still was so much to do. She'd put in many long days already, packing and hauling things to the thrift store or the dump on the far side of the island.

Not that she minded, since staying busy kept her mind off D.J. According to Gram, he'd stopped by Monday night. Aside from that, he could have been on the moon. Liza had heard nothing from him. She hadn't contacted him, either. Facing him Saturday was going to be tough, and she wished there was a way to avoid him. Unfortunately, there was nothing she could do except put on a happy face, and keep it on until he finished helping them and drove away.

But that wasn't her only problem. She glanced at the clock. It was nearly three o'clock and she had yet to hear from the Seattle school district.

This was not a good sign. Feeling genuinely downcast, she blew the hair out of her eyes and turned to her grandmother. "I don't think I got that job in Seattle. The principal would've called by now."

"It's only been three days. I'm sure you'll hear from her soon."

Since she'd specifically said "by Thursday," Liza had her doubts.

"You may as well stop by the Halo Island administration offices and talk to Marsha Devaney," Gram said. "We've been at this for hours, and we both need a break. Why don't you clean up and go over there right now."

Couldn't hurt, especially since Tina had let Marsha know that Liza needed a job. "All right. I'll go change."

To reach the stairs, Liza stepped around a dozen boxes on the living-room floor. Some of them bearing the Island Air logo. D.J.'s contribution.

Gram thought he was sweet and considerate. He was, and honest, too. D.J. Hatcher was a good man, who simply did not love Liza. And why did she keep thinking about him? Her mooning was getting old and tiresome.

She changed into a dress that wasn't too dowdy, then returned to the living room.

"You look nice," her grandmother said. "Good luck, and tell Marsha hello."

Fifteen minutes later, Liza parked in front of the Halo Island administration offices, which shared space with a real estate company downtown. Halo Island Realtors, the company Gram likely would use when she listed her house.

Marsha Devaney, the school administrator, had been with the school forever, since long before Liza had entered first grade. Liza hadn't seen her in ages, but the woman never seemed to change. Plump and looking more grandmotherly than businesslike in a blouse and slacks, her hair in a bun, Marsha widened her eyes when she saw Liza.

For a moment, Liza wondered whether she'd say something about Timothy, that she was sorry or whatever. But Marsha's smile was warm and she didn't mention the matter.

"Why, if it isn't Liza Miller," she said. "How long has it been? You're looking well."

Liza matched her smile. "Thank you. So are you."

"I've been waiting for you to stop by, ever since Tina Chase contacted me."

"Well, here I am. Do you still have that opening for fall semester?"

"We sure do. With so few teachers on the island, it's not exactly easy to fill short-term positions."

It was only fair to tell the truth. "You should know that I'm waiting to hear from Seattle on a job with a continuing contract."

Marsha's face fell. "I appreciate your honesty."

"Maybe I shouldn't apply?"

"Of course you should. Whether or not you work this fall, we would love to have your application on file." She handed Liza the stapled form. "Fill this out. Then, we'll talk."

"All right, I'll bring it back next week." After Gram moved and she had time to work on it.

"You could do that, but why not complete it right now? That'll save you the trip back. You can use the desk over there, and when you're through, I'll interview you."

Why not? Liza sat down at the desk, fished a pen from her purse and began.

WHILE LIZA PACKED the pots and pans into boxes Friday afternoon, she thought about what had happened after her interview the day before and the conversation later with Gram.

"Halo Island schools—Marsha, that is—offered me the job." Liza had wanted badly to take it, even if it was only for one semester. What stopped her was her strong need for love and a family of her own. Which she wasn't going to find on Halo Island.

"I knew they'd like you." Her grandmother had beamed. "That's wonderful, honey. What did you tell them?"

"Marsha knows about my application with Seattle. I asked if I could let her know on Monday. In case I do hear from them."

"That sounds wise," Gram had said, though her smile had dimmed. "Your mother will want to know."

"I don't plan to contact her until I know for sure what I'm doing. Then I'll send an e-mail. With the huge time difference, it's easier." And since there was no telling what Diane would say, e-mail seemed best.

Liza still held out hope for the Seattle position, but in the summer the offices closed at four, and it was after that now. Apparently, the job had gone to someone else.

Suddenly, her cell phone rang. She snatched it from the table. Seattle School District, the LED said. Her heart seemed to rise to her throat.

"It's Seattle," she told Gram.

"This is Liza Miller," she said. In need of privacy, she went out the front door.

Five minutes later, she'd accepted a job offer. A job that only a few weeks ago would have had her jumping with excitement. Now she wanted to cry. And wasn't that silly?

Determined to count her blessings, Liza straightened her posture and returned to the kitchen. "I just accepted the job with Seattle," she said, doing her best to muster a semblance of enthusiasm.

Her grandmother offered a resigned smile. "If that's what you want, I'm happy for you."

"It's a continuing contract with third-graders. Of course I want it."

"You'd better let Marsha know."

"I'll do that right now." Liza made the call.

"I'm pleased for you, but sorry for Halo Island," Marsha said. "You'd really fit in here. If it's all right with you, I'll keep your application on file. In case you change your mind. Ha-ha."

Her disappointment left Liza feeling more glum than ever.

Gram and Marsha wanted her to stay. So did Diane. If only D.J.... *Stop it right now, Liza.* Tight-lipped, she finished packing the pots and pans, while Gram boxed up the spices.

"If it's okay with you, I'll leave here on Monday. But I can come back in a few weeks to help more with this house." When there was some distance between her and D.J., and she had her heart under control.

"You've already done more than enough. Goodness sakes, you have your own life to lead." Gram sighed. "I suppose I'd better call the Realtor."

BY THE TIME D.J. walked to Mrs. Haverford's door Saturday morning, he'd heard that Liza had landed that job in Seattle. She loved teaching as much as he loved flying, so he was glad for her. Even if he did feel like hell.

Love hurt. What else was new? He would do what he'd

promised and move her grandma. Determined to act as if life was great, he rapped sharply on the screen door.

Almost immediately, Liza opened it. Her hair was back in a loose ponytail and her clothes were comfortable and old. Familiar desire grabbed him, and his heart expanded with emotion. Damned if he was about to show his feelings.

"Heard you got the job," he said, trying to look pleased. "Congratulations."

"Thanks." She flashed a smile. "Come in."

"Let's get started," he said. There was no sign of Mrs. Haverford. "Where's your grandma?"

"Somewhere in the back of the house. Thanks for the boxes. It was nice of you to bring them by."

"I figured she needed them." He shrugged. "Why don't I start loading the truck. I'll do the furniture on the next trip." He hefted a carton from the floor. On his way out, so casually he impressed himself, he asked, "When does your new job start?"

"At the end of August." She looked and sounded over-joyed. "But I'm leaving the island on Monday."

"Wow, that's soon."

"I know." She grabbed a box. "I need to find an apartment and get myself moved."

D.J. wanted to be happy for her, but the truth was he felt empty and bleak. And his jaw hurt from faking a smile. "Fantastic," he said. Shouldering open the screen door, he let Liza walk out first, then followed her.

"I'm glad you're so thrilled about it," she said.

She sounded almost sarcastic. Odd.

"That's what friends do. Act happy when other friends get what they want."

"It's what I want, all right," she said, her cheerfulness sounding forced.

Which was even stranger. D.J. squinted at her, but her eyes were on the box in her arms.

"Gonna fly back?" he asked.

"Yes."

"Huh." Hoping to God she wasn't on one of his flights—that would be too damn painful—he set his carton in the bed of the truck. "So your grandma's gonna have to sell the house. That's a crying shame."

He took the box from Liza's hands, his palms brushing her knuckles. For one brief moment her eyes met his. Need and longing overpowered him.

Then she looked away. "I know," she said, but he was too distracted to remember what they were talking about.

It took every ounce of willpower not to curl his hands over hers and pull her close. But she didn't want him anymore, and he wasn't about to make a fool of himself. He cleared his throat, turned away and returned to the house.

They continued to load the truck bed in silence, D.J. careful to keep his distance. Which wasn't all that difficult, since Liza seemed to be doing the same.

Soon the pickup was full, and D.J. was more than ready to put more space between him and Liza.

"I need the key to your grandma's apartment," he said as Mrs. Haverford entered the kitchen.

"Hello, D.J. I didn't know you'd arrived. How long have you been here?"

"Long enough to fill the truck. The first load is ready to go. All I need is your key."

"It's right here." She took it from the windowsill over

the sink. "Do you have room for one more little box from the garage? I'll show you where it is. Liza, will you finish packing up the linens?"

Liza nodded and left the room as if she couldn't wait to get away from D.J. Even though he felt that way, too, that stung.

"You heard that Liza got the job?" Mrs. Haverford said as she took his arm.

"Yep." He pulled his lips into a grin and they began a slow trip to the garage.

"There's a teaching job here on the island," she said, eyeing him with a look he couldn't decipher. "But it's only for one semester. They offered it to Liza. Of course, she turned it down."

"I hadn't heard about that, but it's no surprise. She needs permanent full-time work."

"I know, but I hate for her to go. Don't you?"

D.J. did, but he wasn't about to share that with Liza's grandma. "She got what she wanted, right? That's what matters."

They reached the garage. He glanced around. "Where's that box you want me to take over?"

Mrs. Haverford glanced at an empty shelf, then gave him a small smile. "It was a box of gardening tools for my terrace plants, but it's not here. Maybe Liza packed it with some of the other things. You don't seem happy for her."

The woman was too damn nosy and too damn perceptive. D.J. set his jaw. "Is that what this is about? You're worried that I'm not happy for Liza? Well, I am." He forced a smile. "See? Now I'd best get going, or this move will take forever."

By MIDAFTERNOON Saturday, Gram was moved into her new apartment, more or less. Boxes littered the floor and every table in the small apartment. Liza and D.J. had worked nonstop, first moving, then arranging the furniture according to her directions. Liza had set up the kitchen, too.

The physical labor was tiring in itself, but pretending she felt little for D.J. was downright exhausting for Liza. Though he didn't shoot her warm looks or even talk to her except when necessary. Something about him was different. He acted as if he no longer liked her at all, even as a friend.

Even if she was behaving just as coolly, this new indifference hurt. And also puzzled her. She'd never seen this side of D.J., and she didn't understand it. She sank wearily onto a box.

"I'm all out of energy. I don't think I can do one more thing today." She glanced at D.J., leaning against the wall with his arms crossed, and Gram, inert on the sofa. "I think the three of us are through for the day."

"I certainly am," Gram said. "Why don't you both go home, so this old woman can take a nap. I don't feel like cooking tonight, and isn't it nice that there's a dining room the next building over? If you two would like to join me for dinner…"

Wanting only to be alone and stop pretending, Liza shook her head. "That's sweet, Gram, but I think I'll go back to the house and collapse."

D.J. pushed away from the wall. "I'm beat, too."

He glanced at Liza. His jaw tightened a hair. Nothing a person would notice, unless she knew him as well as Liza did. He seemed angry with her. Who knew why, but his distance was getting old. Even if it was for the best.

"I'll drop you off," he said in a gruff voice.

Clearly, he didn't want to give her a ride. Liza raised her chin. "You've already done enough. I'll call a cab."

D.J. stiffened. "I said I'd drive you."

"And *I* said I'd rather—"

Gram slapped the coffee table with a resounding slap. "Both of you can stop this ridiculous behavior right now!"

Surprised, Liza closed her mouth. D.J. backed up.

Gram gave them both dirty looks. "I don't know what the problem is between you two, but you've been acting like petulant children all day. I'm sick to death of the tension."

She was right. Liza glanced at D.J., who was eyeing Gram.

"Sorry, Mrs. H."

"Me, too," Liza said.

"I'm not the one needing the apologies." Gram looked at Liza. "You let D.J. drive you home, and on the way, you talk and straighten out whatever's happened between you."

"All right." Liza threw up her hands. "I'll bring your car over in the morning, Gram."

"Keep it until Monday." Her grandmother stood. "You can pick me up and I'll drop you at Island Air."

Though Liza's attention was focused on her grandmother, she felt D.J.'s stare. What was he thinking? "Okay, but I'll be over in the morning to help with anything you need."

"All right, anytime after breakfast." Hooking one hand through D.J.'s arm and the other through Liza's, Gram walked them to the door, her outburst already forgotten. "Thank you so much for giving up your Saturday to help Liza and me with this move, D.J. I don't know what we would have done without you."

"No problem. I'd like to think someone would do this for my grandma, too."

His face flushed and the tension left his jaw, and for a moment, again, he looked like the D.J. Liza knew and loved. So that he wouldn't see her feelings, she glanced at the ground.

At the door she kissed Gram's cheek. "Have a nice nap, and call if you need anything."

"I will. See you in the morning. Don't forget about those apologies."

The instant her grandmother shut the door, Liza made hers. "Whatever I did to make you angry, I'm sorry."

"I'm not mad. Why would I be?"

"You seem so…distant."

"And you don't?"

"What do you want me to do, fall all over you?"

The old D.J. would've cracked a joke laced with sexual innuendo. The man beside her simply opened the door for her.

"You're different," she said after he climbed into the driver's seat.

"No, I'm not. You're imagining things." His smile looked convincing enough. He started the engine, and she buckled her seat belt. "My turn to apologize."

"For barely talking to me all day?"

"That goes both ways. Because your grandma asked me to."

"Whatever," Liza muttered.

After a few moments of silence spent with her looking out the passenger window and D.J. dealing with traffic, she glanced at him. "Do you think she'll be happy in that tiny apartment?"

"She seemed excited."

Talking about this neutral subject, some of the tension between them faded.

"It's a big adjustment, and not just for her," Liza said. "It'll feel strange, staying in the house without her and her things." And even more bizarre when people Liza didn't know bought the place and moved in.

"You'll handle it. You're only alone there for the weekend. Then you're out of here."

He sounded so cavalier. She couldn't stop a heavy breath. About to turn onto Treeline Road, D.J. shot her a quizzical look.

"I'm worn out," she said. And heartsick for so many reasons. Her one-sided feelings for D.J. Her grandmother's move. The job in Seattle.

"I hear ya." He took one hand off the steering wheel and started to reach out to her. Then he changed his mind and dropped his hand.

They rode the rest of the way without speaking. At last D.J. signaled and pulled up the driveway.

"Well, thanks again for everything." Liza started to open the door.

"Wait." He touched her upper arm.

Hopeful that maybe he cared after all, she turned to him. "Yes?"

"Enjoy that new job and take care of yourself, all right?" he said in a low, intimate voice.

Words crowded her throat. *I care about you more than any job. Ask me to stay and I will.* But he'd never do that, so she simply replied, "You take care, too. Will you let me know when the partnership is finalized? You have my number and my e-mail address."

"Sure."

His fingers grazed her cheek. Love and warmth filled her. Heaven help her, she leaned into his hand.

"Goodbye, Liza."

His lips brushed hers with tenderness, a brief farewell that made her want to sob.

She swallowed thickly, then offered a brave smile. "Goodbye, D.J."

Feeling bereft and alone, and fighting the urge to beg him to stay, Liza walked into the empty house.

Chapter Fifteen

On a Monday night two weeks after Liza had left the island, D.J. and his employees finalized the details of their partnership. In the morning, his attorney would file the partnership papers.

To celebrate, after Island Air closed for the night, D.J., Joe and the six other partners shared pizza and beer at the Gull's Nest. Even though there was no live music tonight, the place was crowded with locals and tourists.

D.J. couldn't help remembering the last time he'd been in here. Babysitting Kiki and dancing with Liza. He'd started to fall for her that night. He just hadn't wanted to admit it.

People began to leave, until only D.J. and Joe remained.

Joe took one look at him and shook his head. "For a man who should be on top of the world, you're in a sorry state."

He was right. D.J. wasn't as pleased as he should've been. The strange truth was, Island Air wasn't as important to him anymore. Not without Liza. He missed her. Thought about her constantly. The few times he'd called to update her on the company happenings, the conversations had been painfully short and casual.

Proud of the way he hid his feelings, he brightened his expression. "Hey, I feel great. Never better."

"That's the lamest smile ever. Who is she?"

Maybe he wasn't much of an actor. "What are you talking about?" he said.

"Come on, Deej, I've been lovesick myself. Still am, for Brianna. I sure will be glad when she's back on the island again."

D.J. thought about Liza, who was preparing to move from her apartment in Bellingham to a new one in Seattle. When he'd phoned her this afternoon to update her on the partnership, she'd sounded happy and excited about her life. He'd hung up in a funk.

"At least Brianna's coming back," he said.

"Ah. We're talking about Liza Miller."

Joe had flown her to Seattle, which had been a relief to D.J.

"Afraid so." Miserable, D.J. rested his chin on his fist. "I'm in love with her."

"So, it finally happened to you. About time. What are you waiting for, an invitation? Go after her, man."

D.J. was skeptical. "I don't think she wants me."

"You'll never know unless you talk to her."

"Yeah, but rejection hurts. I don't like pain."

"Copy that. But for all the times women have messed up my heart, I've never regretted trying. Heck, if I hadn't put myself on the line, Brianna and I wouldn't be together now."

At home later, D.J. thought about what Joe had said. It made sense. Risky as it was, he knew he had to tell Liza how he felt.

And just how would that work, lunkhead? She's got a new job in Seattle and you live here.

D.J. didn't know the answer to that, or even if there was any hope for a serious relationship with Liza. But he intended to find out.

TUESDAY EVENING Liza was packing up the last of her Bellingham apartment for the next morning's move to Seattle, when someone knocked on the door. Thinking it was her neighbor, who'd helped carry boxes from her second-floor unit to the rented U-Haul and had stayed for takeout, she opened the door with a smile on her face. "What did you forget, Suze?"

Only it wasn't Suze, it was D.J. Hatcher, looking as handsome as ever.

"D.J.," she said, knowing her surprise showed. Despite her best intentions, she loved him more than ever, and after two long weeks away from him her heart thudded joyfully. She ached to lay her palm against his cheek, lean in and kiss him, and it was all she could do to stifle the urge. "What are you doing here?"

"I just flew a group to Seattle, and since my next flight is *from* Seattle first thing in the morning, I figured I'd save time and gas and stick around tonight. So I was in the area…" He shifted his weight. "And I thought I'd stop by."

In the area? With ninety miles separating Bellingham from Seattle, not quite. He wouldn't simply drop in for no reason.

"You didn't say anything when you called yesterday. I wish you'd let me know you were coming." She glanced behind her at the boxes and clutter everywhere. "You know I'm about to move. The place is a disaster." Without makeup, her hair falling out of its ponytail and dressed in grimy old clothes, so was she. But he'd certainly seen her like this before.

"Then I won't look. You gonna invite me in?"

"Of course." She widened the door. A thought occurred to her, and she narrowed her eyes. "I'm unlisted. How did you get my address?"

He wiped his feet on the mat and stepped inside. "From your grandma."

Not an hour ago Liza had spoken with Gram. She'd never said a word. "She knew you were coming?"

"I told her."

How odd of Gram. "My refrigerator is mostly empty, but I think there's a can of pop left. Or how about a glass of water?"

"I'm fine, thanks."

Most of the furniture was loaded in the truck, but there was one kitchen chair left. "Um, have a seat."

"You take it," D.J. said. "I'll stand."

She'd never seen him fidget, but he was now, shifting around, turning down the cuffs of his shirt sleeves, then rolling them up, adjusting the collar of his open-neck shirt.

A sense of foreboding came over her. "You're making me nervous, D.J. Why are you here?"

He stilled. Pulled in an audible breath and exhaled. Cleared his throat. "I wanted to see you."

She opened her mouth to tell him that she was glad, but he held up his hand, silencing her.

"I need to finish this before I chicken out. I know you don't have feelings for me, but if you just…" The words trailed off.

Not knowing what to think, her heart in her throat, Liza leaned forward. "If I just what, D.J.?"

"Oh, hell." He scrubbed his hand over his face. "I had a speech all memorized but I'm no good at that, so I'll just come out and say it. I miss you something awful. Without you, nothing matters. I love you."

The expression on his face—tense expectation mixed with wariness, told her how scared he was. She loved him all the more for opening his heart.

"Then this is your lucky day," she said. "Because I love you, too."

"You do?"

His surprise was so comical, Liza laughed. "I think I started to fall for you that June day you flew me to the island."

"Yeah?"

In an instant she was in his arms, his lips claiming hers for a searing kiss. Liza sank against him.

This was where she belonged.

Moments later, he rested his forehead against hers. "You mean all this time I've been suffering for nothing? Why didn't you say something?"

"Because you specifically said that you did not want to get serious. I was afraid that if I told you how I felt, I'd never see you again."

"What an idiot I was." He sat down on the chair, then tugged her hand and pulled her onto his lap. "All that time we wasted."

"Not really. At first, I wasn't ready. And you certainly weren't, either." She stroked his cheek. "Remember that afternoon on the rock? You were *so* not ready for words of love."

"I guess not." Head tilted, he cupped his ear. "I am now."

Liza leaned in close. "I love you, D.J. Hatcher."

"That's… Wow." A slow grin spread across his face, crinkling the corners of his eyes.

He tipped up her chin and kissed her, a sweet, light press of his lips that quickly turned hot and demanding.

Long, deep kisses later, when Liza was aching with need, D.J. broke contact. His eyes were fevered and his breath labored. "When you feel this way, there's only one thing to do. Let's get married."

Liza had never expected this. She eyed him. "But you don't want to get married ever again. Remember?"

"A man can change his mind, can't he?"

"I want kids, at least three," she tested.

"That sounds like just the right number." He nuzzled her neck. "We could start working on that now, if you want."

His lips made her feel boneless and filled her with yearning. She wanted, all right. At least, her heart did. But her mind raced with the hurdles that remained.

If only he'd spoken up two weeks ago, she'd have turned down the Seattle job for the semester position at Halo Island. Unfortunately, he hadn't.

Reluctantly, she pulled away. "But I've signed a contract. I'm moving to Seattle tomorrow. You live on the island. We can't get married."

His expression darkened. "You're saying you don't want to marry me."

"Oh, but I do, more than you know." She cupped his face between her hands and smiled. "You're the man of my dreams."

D.J. visibly relaxed. "That's all I need to know. I've

been doing some thinking. I could try to run Island Air from Seattle."

"Is that really possible?"

"I don't know," he admitted. "For sure, it would be a real chore—more back and forth, and longer days. And it might not work. But if you're not beside me, nothing else matters. For us, I'm willing to do whatever it takes."

Liza appreciated that. She also had to wonder. She bit her lip. "And if it doesn't?"

"We'll worry about that later."

With D.J. peering intently into her eyes, his face filled with hope, Liza's heart melted. Yet some small part of her feared that he might not be able to run the airline from Seattle. That he'd end up resentful and unhappy. Then where would they be?

"You're my heart, babe." D.J. kissed her again, this time gently and tenderly. And all too briefly. His eyes were misty and lit with feeling. "You're something special. I'd like to show you just how much you mean to me. Please don't tell me you packed the bed."

"I did, but the mattresses are still here." Liza slid off his lap and led him to the bedroom.

Much later, deeply satisfied and filled with love, she propped her arms on D.J.'s chest to look at him. "You know, my roots are on the island. I'd much rather live there. Gram's house hasn't gone on the market yet. How would you feel about moving into it?"

Looking thoughtful, he fiddled with her hair. "You'd give up your job for me? What about that contract you signed?"

"I'm sure there are other qualified teachers who'd like to have the position. As soon as the district offices open in the morning, I'll call and let them know I changed my mind. Maybe that fall-semester teaching job is still open. Marsha said they have trouble filling those slots."

"That'd be awesome."

His relief that he might not have to relocate was visible, and Liza knew that no matter what he'd said before, she could not ask him to move for her.

BEFORE DAWN, D.J. was up and showered. After a night spent sharing plans for the future and making love—and not talking about what would happen if she couldn't get out of her contract—Liza wanted nothing more than to stay in the cozy oasis of love that she and D.J. had created.

"Do you *have* to go?" she asked when he bent down to kiss her goodbye.

"If I don't, there'll be ten unhappy tourists wondering where I am. And I want those passengers to say great things about Island Air and fly us again and again." He smoothed back her hair. "Have I told you lately that I love you?"

"Mmm-hmm," she said. "But tell me again."

"I love you." He kissed her, igniting passion in her.

"Couldn't you stay a little longer?" she teased, licking her lips. "I'll make it worth your while."

His eyes glittered with heat. "Don't tempt me. I'll be back after my last flight this afternoon. You can make it worth my while before we load up the mattresses."

Liza had to be out of the apartment by 6:00 p.m. tonight.

"Call me after you talk to the Seattle school district," D.J. said. "And call your grandma and let her know we want to come see her tomorrow night. That way we can give her the good news in person."

Liza nodded, then shared some of the thoughts that were troubling her. "They might not let me out of my contract, so don't get your hopes up."

"Then, like I said, I'll move to Seattle."

WHEN D.J. WALKED into her apartment later that afternoon, Liza was waiting. It had been a very good day, and except for the mattresses the U-Haul was packed. Her heart was full, and yet the doubts lingered.

"You didn't call, babe." He took her hands and studied her face. "Bad news?"

She shook her head. "I've been saving it to tell you in person. Seattle released me from my contract. The landlord in Seattle is charging me for a month's rent, but he let me break the lease agreement. Best of all, I got the semester teaching job on the island." Her eyes filled. "It's all wonderful."

The happiness on his face turned to concern. "Then why are you crying?"

The fears she'd held in since yesterday gushed out. "I was afraid I'd be stuck working in Seattle." Letting go of his hand, she pulled a tissue from her jeans pocket and blotted the tears. "I never could've asked you to move there for me. It just wouldn't have been fair to you."

Now he looked both surprised and puzzled. "Hey, you didn't ask me to move here, I offered. You ought to know by now that I don't say something unless I mean it." He kissed the tip of her nose. "I'm not like that other guy, babe. I'm here for life."

Through watery eyes, Liza searched his face. She saw nothing but love and commitment there. In her soul she knew that no matter where life took them, they'd grow old together. Smiling through her tears, she twined her arms around his neck. "Oh, D.J., I love you so much."

"Me, too. Forever and ever." He kissed the tip of her nose. "Are we okay now? Anything else you want to talk about?"

She nodded. "When do you want to get married?"

AFTER PACKING the mattresses and leaving the U-Haul at a secured lot in Seattle, Liza and D.J. flew to Halo Island to see Gram. She'd called and told her grandmother they were coming.

Before they could knock on the apartment door, it opened. Gram had been watching for them. "Hello, you two." She drew them inside and engulfed them both in a hug.

When she released them, D.J. was chuckling. "Guess you figured out why we're here."

Gram nodded. "I—"

"Don't say another word," Liza said. "I want Mother and Art to hear everything. They're in Sydney this week, and I just happen to have the number of their hotel."

"It's almost midnight there," Gram said. "They're probably asleep."

"This is important enough to wake them," D.J. said.

Liza made the call and put the phone on speaker.

"Hello?" Diane answered.

"Hi, Mother. It's Liza."

"Something's happened to Mother," she said, sounding worried.

"I'm right here, Diane, and I'm fine," Gram assured her.

Liza caught hold of D.J.'s hand. "D.J.'s here, too. You're on speakerphone."

"Art, get over here," Diane said. "It's Liza, and *D.J.'s* with her."

"Hey there, Diane and Art. Hope you're having a good time." D.J. raised a brow at Liza. She gave him the go-ahead with a nod. "Good news. Liza and I are getting married."

"Art, they're engaged!" Diane said. "How unexpected. How wonderful!"

They heard Art whoop.

Gram laughed. "You can say that again."

"You're not pregnant, are you?"

Only Diane would ask such a question.

"No, Mother." Liza rolled her eyes in irritation. Then D.J. massaged her neck, and she relaxed. "But we are planning to start a family in the next few years."

"I *knew* I should save those children's books from your grandmother's attic. What about your job in Seattle? That continuing contract you e-mailed me about. You sounded so pleased."

"They found a replacement. I'll be teaching here on the island this fall." Liza looked at her grandmother. "D.J. and I would love to live in the house. Unless you changed your mind."

"I wouldn't dream of selling now." Gram beamed. "I'm absolutely thrilled. That house served me well through my marriage and after. May you be as happy in it."

Tears of joy filled Liza's eyes. "We will, Gram."

"Thanks, Mrs. H."

Gram shook her finger at D.J., smiling all the while. "None of that Mrs. H. stuff anymore. Please call me Gram."

Looking pleased, D.J. nodded. "Gram."

"Oh, I like that," she said.

"Hello?" Diane said. "Have you set a date?"

Liza and D.J. looked at each other. "We'd like to get married as soon as our relatives and D.J.'s grandmother can get here. Hopefully before school starts next month."

"You can't get married that fast," Diane said. "People need thirty days' notice. Then there's the cake, the flowers, the entertainment…"

"Relax, Mother. We don't want anything fancy."

D.J. shook his head. "We're keeping things simple. Just the wedding, followed by a small reception for friends and family."

"Are you sure?" Diane said. "Because you can have whatever you want."

"Everything I want is in this room." D.J. put his arm around Liza and pulled her to his side.

In full agreement, she smiled up at him.

"All of a sudden, it's awfully quiet," Diane said. "What's going on over there?"

Gram chuckled. "They're acting like the young lovers they are. I wish you could see they way they're looking at each other."

"I hate that I'm missing that! Art and I can cut our trip short and come back to help you."

That was the last thing Liza wanted. "You're only gone two more weeks. Stay and enjoy yourselves."

"But you're in a hurry. Without me there, who'll see to all the wedding details?"

As usual, Diane had ignored Liza and D.J.'s wish to keep things simple. She wanted to push her own agenda on them, Liza's cue to become frustrated and angry.

But D.J. smiled into her eyes, and she remained calm

and unruffled. Knowing he would always be at her side, keeping her balanced, and grateful for his love and support, she sent him a silent thank-you.

"Did you not hear my question?" Diane said. "There are so many details to be planned. If I'm not there to take care of them, who—"

"We'll manage," Liza said. "It's late in Australia, and we should hang up now."

Gram gave an approving nod. "Good night, Diane. We'll see you in two weeks." She disconnected.

Liza gave her brow a mental swipe. "I'm glad that's over."

"So am I. Would you like to eat with me tonight? The food here is quite good, and I've made some friends I'd like you to meet. And of course, we have a wedding to plan."

Liza wanted nothing but to be alone with D.J., but she hadn't seen her grandmother in two weeks. And she was so pleased.

"That sounds fun," she said, looking at D.J. "Is it okay with you?"

His eyes said he wanted her alone, but he gave an understanding nod. "Sure."

"Wonderful." Gram smiled. "I'll just wash my hands and we'll go."

The instant she disappeared into the bathroom, D.J. pulled Liza into his arms. "Happy?"

She let out a contented sigh. "Extremely."

"And this is just the beginning. We're going to have a wonderful life together."

Liza didn't doubt that for a second.

* * * * *

Enjoy a sneak preview of
MATCHMAKING WITH A MISSION
by B.J. Daniels,
part of the **WHITEHORSE, MONTANA** *miniseries.*
Available from Harlequin Intrigue
in April 2008.

Nate Dempsey has returned to Whitehorse to uncover the truth about his past…

Nate sensed someone watching the house and looked out in surprise to see a woman astride a paint horse just on the other side of the fence. He quickly stepped back from the filthy second-floor window, although he doubted she could have seen him. Only a little of the June sun pierced the dirty glass to glow on the dust-coated floor at his feet as he waited a few heartbeats before he looked out again.

The place was so isolated he hadn't expected to see another soul. Like the front yard, the dirt road was waist-high with weeds. When he'd broken the lock on the back door, he'd had to kick aside a pile of rotten leaves that had blown in from last fall.

As he sneaked a look, he saw that she was still there, staring at the house in a way that unnerved him. He shielded his eyes from the glare of the sun off the dirty window and studied her, taking in her head of long blond hair that feathered out in the breeze from under her Western straw hat.

She wore a tan canvas jacket, jeans and boots. But it was the way she sat astride the brown-and-white horse that nudged the memory.

He felt a chill as he realized he'd seen her before. In that very spot. She'd been just a kid then. A kid on a pretty paint horse. Not this one—the markings were different. Anyway, it couldn't have been the same horse, considering the last time he had seen her was more than twenty years ago. That horse would be dead by now.

His mind argued it probably wasn't even the same girl. But he knew better. It was the way she sat the horse, so at home in a saddle and secure in her world on the other side of that fence.

To the boy he'd been, she and her horse had represented freedom, a freedom he'd known he would never have— even after he escaped this house.

Nate saw her shift in the saddle, and for a moment he feared she planned to dismount and come toward the house. With Ellis Harper in his grave, there would be little to keep her away.

To his relief, she reined her horse around and rode back the way she'd come.

As he watched her ride away, he thought about the way she'd stared at the house—today and years ago. While the smartest thing she could do was to stay clear of this house, he had a feeling she'd be back.

Finding out her name should prove easy, since he figured she must live close by. As for her interest in Harper House… He would just have to make sure it didn't become a problem.

* * * * *

Be sure to look for
MATCHMAKING WITH A MISSION
and other suspenseful Harlequin Intrigue stories,
available in April
wherever books are sold.

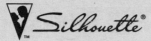

Silhouette®

Romantic
SUSPENSE

Sparked by Danger,
Fueled by Passion.

The Taken

Tierney Doyle is used to being criticized for
her psychic abilities, yet the tough-as-nails—
and drop-dead-gorgeous—detective has no doubt
about what she has uncovered in the case of a
string of unsolved murders. And Tierney is slowly
discovering that working so close to her partner,
detective Wade Callahan, could be lethal.

Look for

Danger Signals
by Kathleen Creighton

Available in April wherever books are sold.

REQUEST YOUR FREE BOOKS!
2 FREE NOVELS PLUS 2
FREE GIFTS!

American ★ Romance®

Heart, Home & Happiness!

HAR08

HARLEQUIN®

Super Romance®

Celebrate the joys of motherhood!
In this collection of touching stories,
three women embrace their maternal
instincts in ways they hadn't expected.
And even more surprising is how true
love finds them.

Mothers of the Year

With stories by
Lori Handeland
Rebecca Winters
Anna DeStefano

Look for Mothers of the Year,
available in April
wherever books are sold.

      HSR71482

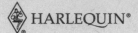

HARLEQUIN®

American ★ Romance®

COMING NEXT MONTH

#1205 RUNAWAY COWBOY by Judy Christenberry
The Lazy L Ranch
Jessica Ledbetter has worked too hard on her family's dude ranch to let
Jim Bradford, a cowboy turned power broker and the ranch's new manager,
show her up. The Lazy L is Jess's legacy, and she isn't about to let it fall into
the hands of an outsider. No matter what those hands can do to her...

#1206 MARRYING THE BOSS by Megan Kelly
When Mark Collins finds himself in a competition with Leanne Fairbanks for
the position of CEO of the family business, he can't believe it. But as they go
head-to-head in a series of tasks to fight for the top job, Mark begins to see her
as more than just a rival. And if he wins, will he lose *her*?

#1207 THE MARRIAGE RECIPE by Michele Dunaway
Catching her fiancé in bed with one of the restaurant's curvaceous employees
sends up-and-coming pastry chef Rachel Palladia fleeing Manhattan for the
comforts of home. But when her ex threatens to sue for her dessert recipes, she
turns to her high school heartthrob, Colin Morris, who happens to be the town
lawyer—and he's a lot sweeter than revenge!

#1208 DOWN HOME DIXIE by Pamela Browning
No real Southern belle would fall for a Yankee—especially not one named
Kyle Sherman. But Dixie Lee Smith does, and hides the truth about his
illustrious ancestor from her family. What's worse, as soon as she finds out
she's got competition, *she* goes to war—to keep the handsome Northerner
for herself!

www.eHarlequin.com